TWENTIETH CENTURY FOX Presents
A KINGS ROAD ENTERTAINMENT Production of
A WOLFGANG PETERSEN Film
DENNIS QUAID   LOUIS GOSSETT, JR.
ENEMY MINE
Music by MAURICE JARRE
Director of Photography TONY IMI, B.S.C.
Executive Producer STANLEY O'TOOLE
Screenplay by EDWARD KHMARA
Based on the Story by BARRY LONGYEAR
Produced by STEPHEN FRIEDMAN
Directed by WOLFGANG PETERSEN

Special Effects by ILM

 DOLBY STEREO ^R
IN SELECTED THEATRES

© 1985 Twentieth
Century Fox

ENEMY MINE

Barry B. Longyear and David Gerrold
From the screenplay by Edward Khmara
Based on the story by Barry B. Longyear

**Now a sensational New Movie
from Twentieth Century Fox**

Ⓒ CHARTER BOOKS, NEW YORK

ENEMY MINE

A Charter Book/published by arrangement with
the authors and 20th-Century Fox

PRINTING HISTORY
Charter edition/December 1985

ISBN: 0-441-20672-7

Charter Books are published by The Berkley Publishing Group,
200 Madison Avenue, New York, New York 10016.
PRINTED IN THE UNITED STATES OF AMERICA

For Bill W. and Dr. Bob

1

THE OUTER-PERIMETER SATELLITE probe had forty-three seconds to report the approach of the enemy marauders before it was destroyed. It was more than enough warning.

Even before confirmation was logged at the Starbase, the klaxon was sounding throughout the corridors of the flight deck. Ready crews scrambled out of the way as pilots came charging down the hall and into the launch bay. Major Anne Morse's Wednesday Group was leading the pack.

Davidge's ship, *The Shrike*, was third in line. Davidge hauled himself into his cockpit, counting automatically as he did. His navigator Joe Wooster—young, blond, an eager beaver—was already two beats ahead. Wooster held up one forefinger to show he would wait for Davidge to catch up before resuming his own count.

Davidge plugged his suit into the ship's controls, sealed his helmet, punched for ready-check, sealed the cockpit, shouted "Resume count," punched for ship-check, waited for his board to clear green and fastened his harness-web into position. The screen in front of him was already displaying vector: TARGET MANEUVER—DROP TO ANGLE 36 MARK 6. STAND BY FOR INTERCEPT—OVER THE POLE OF FYRINE IV.

Something underneath them clanged shut: The ready crews had just disconnected the last of the umbilicals.

The fighter jerked and slid forward into the launch tube. There was an instant of darkness and free fall as the six BTA fighters dropped away from the Starbase in silence—there was a six-count and then all of their engines ignited simultaneously.

The acceleration pressed Davidge and Wooster deep into their couches. The screaming roar of the rockets vibrated through the entire fighter. It was a deep, visceral, almost sexual, sensation.

And then their engines shut off again. They coasted in free fall. Davidge punched the turbo-drive into readiness.

Before him, his screen blanked, then came up charting. Wooster was already targeting.

"Tally, Flightleader," said Davidge into his helmet-mike. "This is Echo Two. I have bandits at three o'clock."

Major Anne Morse's voice came crackling back: "Roger, Echo Two. I copy. Right ninety and go for it!"

Still coasting, the six fighters angled right and then even farther right; interception was going to be tricky, but not impossible. The fighter's forward motion would have to be cancelled—that vector would have to be added to their intercept vector. And every time the enemy ships changed course, the vectors would be recomputed.

The engines fired and Davidge was pressed back into his couch again. "Turbo-drive . . . *Now!*" shouted Morse. And everything went red and then gray and then they came over the north pole of the planet in a flying wedge.

Fyrine IV was luminous and gray, streaked with white and blue and brown. Its atmosphere was a murky, muddy mess. From space, this world didn't have enough character to even earn a nickname. It was "just another shit-ball."

Davidge's screen showed the enemy as four distinct

blips now. Joe Wooster reported crisply, "They're diving into the atmosphere."

"That won't help 'em."

Simpson's voice came over the radio: "Echo Six to Flightleader. Our buddies are pulling the yellow line."

"All right Wednesday Group, let's take 'em down."

Davidge looked over to the right to see if Arnold was peeling off and diving, but Arnold was already out of visual range.

Wooster said, "Come on, Willy! Let's snuff these bastards and go home early. I got a hot date with Murcheson." His voice cracked on the last word, betraying his nervousness.

Davidge was too busy studying his screen to notice Wooster's fear. He didn't like the way the Dracs had dived for the surface, it was too deliberate. Could they have come up with a new strategy? But he heeled the ship over anyway.

As they came around to their new course he said, "Did I hear you say something about Murcheson? The nurse?"

Wooster grunted agreement. "This time it's gonna happen. She's gonna give in. I know it."

"Lucky man," said Davidge. "Say, isn't that the same Murcheson we used to call, 'the White Walrus'?"

"Hey! Come on! She's lost twenty pounds!"

Davidge grinned. "Have you looked behind her?"

"Hey!" Wooster retorted. "I like a woman with upholstery. It makes for a more comfortable ride."

"Ahh—if you say so." Davidge wasn't paying attention any more. He was watching the heat buildup on the fighter's skin. The Dracs had figured out early that the BTA lasers were useless in the muddy soup of Fyrine IV, and the range of the Terran missiles was more than halved because they had to fight the planet's gravity as well as steer. It almost evened up the odds because once in the atmosphere the BTA fighters had to approach so close to fire their missiles that it gave the Dracs a chance to fire back. Davidge didn't like it. It made for too many things to worry about.

Besides, he didn't like having to fly at atmospheric speeds. It was too slow, too much like being a sitting target. If they were going to take these Dracs out, they'd have to catch them before they hit the soup.

Davidge frowned and eased up on the throttle, shifting the fighter's course high to catch a Drac that was climbing to cross his path. Now, why in hell...? There wasn't time to wonder about it. Three seconds, two seconds—

Almost without thinking, Davidge released two missiles and rolled the ship over sideways. The blast turned the sky white, even though they were facing away from it.

"Whoop!" screamed Wooster in reaction.

Davidge had other things on his mind besides screaming. That blast had been awfully close. He glanced at his screens. "Recalibrate?"

"We're fine," Wooster managed to say. His breathing was definitely unsteady. Then he added, "Well, maybe a little cooked—but I didn't want to have any children anyway."

"Good. Do a favor for the genetic heritage of the species."

"Oh, shit," said Wooster abruptly.

Before Davidge could ask, his screen blinked to show a larger scan. Six more Drac marauders were dropping down into the atmosphere behind them.

"Six more bandits!"

So that was the trick! Okay, it'd be rough, but they could handle it. Davidge thumbed a button. "Leader, copy that?"

Morse's voice came back quickly, "Roger, Echo Two. I guess they thought we didn't see 'em."

"I sure as hell didn't see 'em," Davidge growled. "Did *anybody* see 'em?"

"When we get back," said Morse, "I'm going to have a word with . . ."

"I see 'em now," said Cates.

Davidge's screen showed the BTA fighters angling around to meet the diving Dracs—and for just the briefest instant he let himself doubt that they were actually going to make it back at all.

2

AND THEN he didn't have time to think.

Cates's first missile took out one of the marauders. The flash filled the sky with colored lightning. The residual bursts coruscated across the night, flickering and crackling as they discharged their still-dangerous energies. In other circumstances the view might have been impressive. Right now, Davidge wasn't interested.

"Willy!" That was Wooster. "Bandit on zero!" It was dropping down from above.

Davidge was already pulling the ship into a hard bank to the right. The horizon tilted, turned, but the marauder pilot had outguessed him. The Drac had begun his bank even before Davidge! He was still dropping down toward them, gaining!

"Shit! Hold on to your lunch!" Davidge closed his eyes—even he didn't want to see this—and pulled on the throttle, deliberately rolling the ship sideways. He was risking a stall—or worse. But it was a necessary feint. He counted to one-half, then pulled up hard, hit the red button and climbed. The fighter jumped like a rabbit, screeching like a bar of red-hot metal. Davidge opened his eyes and pulled the ship over backward, upside-down, angling down now, leveling, and then slightly to the right again. This could only work if it was true that the reptilian Drac pilots had distinctly slower reflexes than humans. He wasn't sure—

It had worked. There was the Drac marauder, right in front of them. And in front of the marauder was Echo Six! Simpson.

"Echo Six. Bandits closing."

"Where is he, Wil—"

Everything went blue! Davidge's heart popped. "Oh, sweet Jesus!" screamed Wooster. Davidge heard it as if from a great distance. He was frozen. They were surrounded by blue lightning. This was the closest he'd ever been to a blast. They were probably dead and didn't know it yet. Despite the roaring, despite the crackling, the ship felt curiously silent. He felt like he was coasting through ice-water.

And then the last of the blueness flickered away, and there was the marauder still ahead of him. Not trying to evade. The Drac pilot must have taken it even worse.

Davidge didn't have any anger left. It had burned off with the blue lightning. So had his fear. All that was left was a solitary core of purpose: Kill that Drac. There was no passion, no emotion at all. He had become a death-robot. He dived for the marauder.

"Wooster?"

"Yeah?"

"We got K's left?"

"Another sixty-five and we'll have a heat problem."

"Piece of cake," said Davidge. Even though he knew it wasn't.

The marauder was dropping like a stone. Another two minutes and he'd be lost in the rippling layers of murk that Fyrine IV used as atmosphere. As Davidge closed on him, he began warbling his ship from side to side.

"Never seen 'em do that before," said Wooster.

"It's called a skywalk. It means he's got a busted stabilizer." Davidge replied. "It's gonna make him harder to hit."

Davidge's finger tightened on the trigger and for just the sheerest of moments, he felt somehow linked to the pilot of the marauder—linked in death as well as life. He squeezed. "Say your prayers, Toad-face..." It was almost affectionate.

The missile streaked away, leaving a white trail in the air.

The marauder warbled sideways—

—and the missile streaked past and down into the atmosphere.

"He musta said his prayers," said Wooster.

"Shut up."

The marauder heeled over and dove straight down.

Davidge followed.

3

"WHAT THE HELL are you doing?" Wooster was screaming.

Davidge grunted. "It's not in the manual. I'm making it up."

"Engine heat is climbing! And the shields are going red."

The planet was above them now, it was an illusion, they were diving up into it—they were upside-down. It didn't matter. Davidge couldn't let go of the marauder, it warbled tauntingly ahead of them. What was that pilot doing? Davidge squeezed off two more missiles.

The Drac was already turning sideways, twisting away—the missiles dropped past and disappeared into the distance, the flashes of their explosions echoed back a moment later.

"Come on, Willy, blast him and let's get outta here!"

"Shut up, Joey!" Davidge was trying to concentrate on the Drac. "Just . . . give . . . me . . . one . . ."

And then, there it was. The marauder was sliding almost deliberately into the target zone of Davidge's display.

". . . last . . ."

Davidge squeezed the trigger.

". . . shot!"

The last missile streaked away—it looked like it was going to hit. The Drac was warbling, wobbling. The

9

missile puffed, and then it blossomed blue and white. The Drac ship was silhouetted against the explosion— *they'd missed!*—and then it went bouncing and skittering off sideways, out of control!

"Damn it!" What was wrong with the missiles anyway?!! Was it the soup of Fyrine IV, or what?

The marauder was disappearing into the hazy distance ahead of them. Davidge couldn't tell if smoke was pouring out its wings or if it was simply cutting a wake through the murky air. No, they were still too high— they had to be. That wake had to be smoke. Maybe he could catch the Drac yet and cut him up with the lasers. He angled down after it.

Almost immediately, the ship was buffeting—bouncing and slapping around like a ping-pong ball in a wind tunnel.

"We're hitting the atmosphere! Hard!" Wooster screamed.

Dammit again! They were lower than he'd thought. That was why the missiles had failed. The buffeting grew worse—Davidge began to curse as he fought it. He'd miscalculated, but it didn't matter. They were dead anyway. Wooster hadn't figured it out yet, but Davidge knew it. They'd been dead since they'd flown into the trap. The whole squadron was probably gone by now. They were probably the last. There was only one thing left to do. Take the bastard with you. The buffeting was easing now, but that wasn't a good sign. Where was the marauder? He had to find it. He fired his laser—one quick burst—and whispered quietly, a message for the unseen Drac, "When you get to Hell, tell 'em Davidge sent you."

"Huh?" asked Wooster. "What was that?"

"Nothing!" Davidge pushed the throttle forward and pointed the ship into the buffeting—and then they were stable again. And that was bad news too. It meant that they were *deep* into the soup. There were clouds rushing past them now. Davidge could see nothing.

"I lost him," he said. "What's on the scope?"

"Willy! For God's sake, pull up! We're gonna burn up! We're over the red line now!"

"Where is he?!!"

Something flickered in the distance: Davidge didn't even have a chance to realize what it was; his ship was already disintegrating around him.

No, it wasn't! They'd been *ejected!* Automatically. The Drac must have fired a missile—

Something made him look up, out—it wasn't a missile, the Drac marauder had suicided into the BTA fighter at a speed so fast no human reflex could have acted in time. A blossom of fire was spreading across the sky!

Davidge wanted to laugh—they'd cheated the bastard! The BTA computer had spit out the pilot and navigator in a last desperate act of cybernetic sacrifice. Their life-support capsule was dropping down through the clouds like a stone!

"Joey?"

There was no answer from behind him.

"Joey! Make a noise!"

Davidge tried to twist in his seat to look, but he couldn't tell if Wooster was alive or dead. He'd have to wait until they hit ground.

The first of the drop-chutes opened up, caught them, slowed them and ripped away in the wind. The second chute opened up then, caught the air and billowed, held them even longer before ripping away.

Damn! This soup was thick! How high were they anyway? The capsule's glide-chute finally opened up—a wide wing-shaped affair—and Davidge's controls came back to life in his hands. He steered the capsule around in a wide lazy spiral downward.

The clouds parted as they circled down in dusky silence. The sunlight slanted sideways across the suddenly peaceful world. They hung beneath an ocher ceiling, circling above another layer of clouds, this one pink and rosy. There were clouds above, clouds below—and they were suspended, spiraling, in a layer of clear yellow air.

Davidge squinted into the distance—

—and there across the billowing sea of clouds, far off on the horizon, caught in the last brilliant rays of the Fyrine day, was a single bright speck—a flowering parachute! And beneath it, dark and ominous, a spherical alien capsule!

The Drac had survived too!

Davidge's eyes narrowed against the glare as he angled the capsule around. There wasn't a lot of maneuverability to one of these things, but a good pilot could still fly.

There was no question about it. Davidge had to come down as close as he could to that Drac capsule, find it, find the worm-eating lizard inside it and finish the job he'd been trained to do.

4

THEY CAME OUT of the clouds above a ragged waste-land—cratered and rocky.

"Oh, shit."

Davidge yanked hard on the controls. If he could find a thermal, he could cruise. He could *search*. Otherwise he'd have to use up some of the precious energy in the capsule's life-support system to drive the makeshift craft. The capsule could not function as a real aircraft for long, but the glide-chute provided lift enough to neutralize its fall, and the two steering thrusters on the bottom of the capsule could be used as emergency engines for steering and even a limited amount of climb.

But the surface of the planet was too rocky, too inhospitable. It looked about as friendly as a tax collector's smile. The main priority was going to have to be a safe landing somewhere. Anywhere. The ground seemed to level off up ahead.

"Okay, baby, just give me a few more minutes in the air, that's all I ask for." He thumbed one of the thrusters to life.

Something clicked underneath him. Then it crackled and flickered. There was a bright flash, and then for a moment, silence—

"Nice timing," muttered Davidge. His controls had gone dead in his hands. "Thanks, baby." The capsule was gliding silently toward a jagged ridge. "I'm gonna remember this."

Davidge hit the control for the other thrustor. It coughed, belched and then exploded!

For a moment they were weightless; behind him, Wooster grunted in surprise—*he was alive!*—and then the glide-chute caught again, jerked them, jerked them again, pointed them momentarily upward. The capsule narrowly missed the top of the ridge.

And then they were sliding along the rough sandy ground—sliding and bouncing! The parachute collapsed and then caught again, pulling them along. Davidge punched angrily at the release but nothing happened. The capsule rolled over once, twice, again. The parachute harness caught on something, an outcrop of rock, and the chute collapsed again, this time for good—but the capsule kept rolling. It jerked as the harness caught it and pulled it around. Something was burning—and Wooster was screaming in pain!

"Hang on, Joey!" The capsule was slammed sideways up against a jagged tooth of granite. The world was tilted on its ear. The capsule was flickering and smoking with electric energies. There was an acrid smell in the air.

Davidge slammed the manual release of the canopy. It exploded off and banged across the rocks, skipping and bouncing like a stone across water. Davidge released his safety harness and dropped, slid downward, then climbed sideways and pulled himself up and out of the capsule. He scrambled back a few feet and reached back up into the capsule for the release on Joey's harness. The limp mass of his navigator slid wetly down on top of him.

Davidge grabbed and pulled, grabbed and pulled Joey Wooster across the rocks, away from the crackling, sputtering wreck of their life-support capsule. He pulled him to his feet and they staggered forward together until they toppled and fell over a narrow ridge and rolled, tumbling all the way down a shallow slope and into a rocky gully.

Behind them, the sky turned orange, then white, then orange again—the capsule had exploded. The shock wave slammed over them like a hot steamroller of air. Bits of rock and hot metal pattered down all around them.

Davidge lifted his head. Wooster was covered in grease and blood. He'd lost his helmet somewhere.

Davidge rolled him over on his back. "Joey?"

"Take . . . take off your helmet, Willy. I can't see you." Wooster's eyes looked glassy and unfocused.

Davidge's faceplate was already cracked. He sniffed the air—something smelled burnt—then pulled his helmet off and tossed it aside. He brought his face close to his navigator's again. "Is that better, Joey?"

"Yeah . . ."

"How do you . . ." Davidge was afraid to ask. "How do you feel?"

Joey tried to swallow, coughed instead. "I don't." He added, "Willy?"

"Yeah?" Davidge leaned in closer. Joey's voice was fading.

"When you see Murcheson . . . please don't . . ." he coughed again. "Please don't call her 'the White Walrus' anymore. It hurts her feelings."

"Okay, Joey."

"And . . . and don't let the guys call her that. I liked her."

"That's a promise, Joe."

"I'm tired, Willy. I'm really tired."

"Yeah, Joey—I know."

Behind them, there was a noise—another explosion, this one much smaller. Davidge threw himself across his navigator to protect him. When the rocks and dirt stopped spattering down around them, he lifted himself up and looked down again into Joey Wooster's face.

Joey's eyes stared back at him blankly.

"Joey?"

Davidge put his hand on Joey's chest. "Joey?" He felt nothing. He moved his fingers up to Joey's neck and placed them gently along the line of his carotid artery. There was nothing. No pulse.

The anger rose in Davidge like a scream. "Joey! Dammit! Joey, don't do this! Joey!"

The wind whipped his words away like the last flimsy scraps of the parachute. There wasn't even an echo.

And the night came down, and it was cold and long.

5

DAWN CAME LIKE A WARNING.

The eastern sky turned red, then yellow, then gray. And then the whole sky turned gray and stayed that way all day. Fyrine climbed into the sky and became a brooding red glow behind the clouds.

The ground was rocky and black—except where it was sandy and gray. Gnarled things that looked like trees but weren't, scrabbled for purchase against the continual wind. Blue lichen huddled against the lee side of boulders.

Davidge placed the last of the rocks on Wooster's grave. He wasn't satisfied. The grave was too shallow. The ground had been too hard to dig, even using Joey's helmet as a shovel. And there weren't enough loose rocks to pile around the body. But it was the best he could manage and it would have to do.

He placed Joey Wooster's scorched helmet at the head of the grave, anchoring it carefully, then straightened up brushing his hands against his pants, and took a sad step back to survey his handiwork. He knew he should say something now, but he couldn't find the words. His throat hurt.

Instead, he stood there silently and let the tears stream down his cheeks, streaking his face with dirt. He stood there and wept until he was numb and empty inside— and that, at least, was better than the pain.

Finally he turned away and headed down the rocky slope in the direction he thought the Drac capsule might have come down.

The land dropped away steadily toward the west. There were craters everywhere and smoke still drifted from cracks in the lava. The sharp rocks cut at his hands and boots and an acrid, oily smell made breathing difficult. Davidge began to curse as he walked, a steady litany of offensives against God and man—the mind, body, and morality of each: God for having created a world such as this and creatures like the Drac, and man for being so stupid as to test God's idiocy.

Davidge cursed until he had exhausted himself in all three languages he knew; then he began making up new curses. It seemed to help. He picked his way across the cracked and broken surface of Fyrine IV, embroidering each step with invectives against those who shared the responsibility for this war, this battle and this world.

It was the black plume of smoke that caught his eye first.

Far off, on the edge of the horizon, stood a single upright column of smoke. At its top, the wind whipped it away to nothingness, but at its base it was thick and oily.

"Are you still alive, you motherless reptile?" Davidge eyed the distant plume with a murderous glare. "I hope you are," he whispered to himself. "Because I'm going to spit in your eye, and them I'm going to . . ." He started scrabbling down the slope again. He didn't need to finish the sentence. To hell with cursing, he had something new to think about now.

Now he would think about all the different ways he could kill that goddamn lizard pilot.

There were more of the tree-things down here. They looked like claws piercing upward through the soil, as if something old and evil was trying to escape from the bowels of the planet. They clustered in thickets and looked like cages. They scraped the sky and looked like gallows.

The forest grew thicker as he walked. The trees grew larger now, rising black and dead-looking toward the sky. They arched overhead like the ruins of a cathedral, a ruin of time, left for the ghosts and the ghouls. The hot winds whipped against him, blowing stinging particles of sand into his eyes and his mouth, sucking the moisture from his body and scouring at his skin.

Davidge kept on. He didn't care. He was dead already. He didn't mind. He knew that the universe was only letting him continue because there was still a job to do. A cleanup job. There was a piece of lizard-slime that had to be killed. Davidge couldn't die until he'd finished his job. That was all. It was that simple. He kept on going.

He stumbled through the stark terrain until, exhausted and weak with thirst, he could go no further. He staggered sideways, turned and tripped and fell into a hollow beneath a rocky overhang, and there he took shelter from the wind.

He only meant to rest for a little while—just for a few moments—and then he'd go on; but even his body betrayed him now. He closed his eyes and he was gone.

His sleep was deep and dreamless.

6

THE LAND CONTINUED to drop away. It sloped steadily downward, and Davidge staggered through it like a zombie.

He hardly noticed when the forest gave way to desert.

It was only when he reached the edge of a plateau that he realized how far he'd come. He stopped to survey the land ahead before climbing down.

The red sun gave the land a hellish cast. It looked like a graveyard. It was strewn with boulders the size of tombstones. It stretched off toward a distant crater wall that looked like a massive black mausoleum.

And there in the center of it, not too far ahead, a glint of metal!

The Drac escape capsule!

Davidge stood where he was for a long moment, just staring at the craft, memorizing its location, the landmarks around it. Once he was down in those rocks, he could be lost in moments. He'd have to remember that notch in the crater wall ahead. He could use that as a course marker—and that broken rock that looked like a hunched-over crone, it pointed straight at the wreckage. That would work too.

Davidge unholstered his pistol and checked the charge. He still hadn't decided whether he would make this quick and painless or whether he would— No, it had to be quick and painless. That was what made humans better than lizards; humans had a sense of mercy.

He reholstered his pistol and began climbing down.

The rocky desert was even harder going than the lava fields he had left behind, and Davidge was weaker now. But he didn't care. He was almost there. The job was almost finished. He could see the notch in the distant crater wall, and if he climbed to the top of a rock there were places where he could see the crone and even the wreckage straight ahead. He moved onward, trying to be as silent as he could. The sand scrunched beneath his feet; he slowed his steps to quiet the sound.

By his figuring he still had a ways to go when he came around a boulder and there was the wreckage of the Drac ejection capsule right in front of him. It gleamed brightly in the dull gray light of Fyrine's long day.

Davidge stood there in surprise, breathing raggedly through his mouth, staring in startlement and wonder. Then he remembered his pistol and rapidly pulled it from his holster. He looked around quickly.

This part of the ejection pod had broken into pieces on impact. It still smouldered in places from the explosion of its landing. A fuel cell? Davidge wondered. Or a rocket engine? He hadn't paid too much attention to the various analyses of the Drac marauder's survival abilities. He hadn't ever intended to leave survivors.

Davidge stepped forward cautiously. It didn't look as if anything was hiding in the charred ruin, but he wasn't taking any chances. Not this close.

Only one section of the craft was still recognizable as being a part of a spacecraft; it was a piece of the hull. There were several fuel pods still attached to the inner curve of the metal. All of them were ruptured except one; they leaked and hissed and spat a foul-smelling liquified gas. It spattered on the ground and boiled away in clouds of steam.

A sound! Davidge whirled. Something had *splashed!*

He froze, listening.

No, nothing.

He took a step, then another—the sound had come from *that* direction. Maybe.

He clambered up along a stretch of rock—no, rocky cliffs. The wind plucked at his flight suit.

Splash!

Yes! Water! And something moving in it!

Davidge crept to the edge of the cliff. Slowly . . . He kept himself flat against the rock and edged carefully forward. He held his pistol ready before him. He edged forward again and looked down over the rocks.

Black water! A lagoon! The Fyrine sun was settling over an endless plain that looked like a dried out seabed. In the lee of the cliff below, the green water shimmered. Nearby, a driftwood campfire was smouldering—

—and next to the fire was the rest of the escape pod, intact! The life-support section was a shining metal sphere, sitting lopsided in a sandy furrow. It must have bounced forward, over the cliffs, when the rest of the ejection pod had crashed.

But nothing moved. Except for the crackling fire, there was no sign of life.

Davidge unfolded a pair of electronic binoculars from his belt and scanned the area.

No. Nothing.

Where was the goddamn lizard?!!

He was almost ready to stand up, to climb down to the lagoon, when something caught his attention. A sound.

Bubbles—movement on the water. A small cluster of bubbles rising to the surface.

Davidge focused his binoculars.

Stillness on the water—then, in another place, another cluster of bubbles . . .

. . . and then, something rising, something smooth and sleek, barely breaking the surface of the water, then vanishing again.

Davidge held his breath—

And then there it was, coming out of the water, naked, walking erect. It was taller than a man. Its body was lean and stringy with odd flickering shades of oily color gleaming on its dark skin. Its clawed, three-fingered hands swung at its sides. Davidge could not see its face.

He lowered his binoculars, eased the pistol back into his hand and sighted carefully at the Drac.

Damn.

It was too far away.

The Drac walked to its life-support capsule and pulled the hatch open, took something out, and hunched down near the fire. Davidge raised his binoculars again.

The lizard was eating. Davidge couldn't see clearly what the lizard was eating, but he could see that it was eating *something*. It held the food up to its mouth with both hands and bit at it with tiny bites. It chewed methodically—almost thoughtfully. The goddamn lizard was eating!

Davidge's stomach twisted in reaction. Disgust mixed with hunger.

He lowered the binoculars and licked his dry lips. Once he killed the Drac, the lagoon and the food would be his. He might survive this after all.

He'd have to move closer first. He tucked his pistol back into its holster and began creeping down.

There was a jut of cliff here folded back on itself to form a rocky escarpment. The top of it was almost directly above the lizard. If he could climb over that way—

But the rock was smooth, too smooth. And slippery—

as if it had been polished underwater. Davidge dug in his fingers. He wedged the toes of his boots into the rocks and began to climb.

By the time Davidge reached the edge of the escarpment, his legs were trembling and his fingers were numb. But he had the Drac in range now. The lizard, oblivious to any threat, was still quietly eating.

Davidge eased the pistol into his hand. He took careful aim—

7

HIS FOOT LOST ITS HOLD! He was slipping! His legs scrabbled for purchase. He hung by one hand, his other hand flailing desperately for a grip. The pistol clattered down the rocks and splashed somewhere below.

The Drac leapt to its feet in alarm, its yellow eyes widening in alarm as it peered into the gloom of dusk. It moved its head from side to side in quick, jerky movements, like a bird or a snake. Rage and fear flickered across its face.

Had it turned, it would have seen Davidge, hanging in the air on the curve of the cliff.

The Drac turned—*the other way*—and reached into its capsule and rummaged around for something.

Davidge grabbed for the rock and caught it. He inched his way sideways as quickly and quietly as he could.

The Drac straightened up again with a rifle in its hands. Holding the rifle at ready, it peered around its camp again, but it did not move away from the campfire. Davidge held motionless. *I am a rock. I am a rock.* After a long slow look around, the lizard decided there was nothing unusual hiding in the night, it must have been a rock. The Drac moved back to its place by the fire and squatted down again, its rifle cradled in its arms. It went motionless.

Davidge finished his second count to one thousand and then began to inch his way along the stone until he was wedged into a damp cleft. He allowed himself a silent sigh of relief.

Time passed.

Davidge rested. He had to think. The pistol was in the pool. What else could he use?

What he really needed to do *first* was take care of his thirst. And his hunger.

The Fyrine night was bright. Too bright. Were there moons above those clouds? Or were the clouds luminous? Or did they simply refract the sun's rays around the curve of the planet? Or was there some *other* explanation?

All he had now was his knife. Could he kill the lizard with that?

The clouds were thickening overhead. The air smelled wet and murky. It was time to move. Davidge began to creep along the rock. Thunder rolled in the distance.

Davidge froze!

The Drac was moving. It crossed to its capsule, opened it and began to pull out parts—pieces of control panels and wiring. Davidge couldn't see what it was doing with the components. It didn't make sense. Then the Drac left its rifle protruding from the capsule and walked away.

What the hell—? Was it a trap?

Above, the storm clouds were thickening. The air smelled like water now. The rocks were damp to the touch. A flash of crimson lightning illuminated the landscape like a spark of hell. The thunder rolled and crashed.

The Drac was eating again.

Davidge groaned soundlessly.

His throat hurt, his legs hurt, his arms hurt, his back hurt, his eyes hurt. Most of all, his soul hurt. This wasn't fair. This wasn't right. Why should the goddamn Drac have survived with all that food?

Everything had gone wrong, almost from the start.

He'd even lost his pistol. What else could happen to him now?

Thunder rolled across the sky.

And then it started to rain.

Big warm drops began to pelt him, splattering the cold rocks around him and draining away in rivulets. Soon it was coming down in torrents, splashing out of the clouds like a waterfall.

Davidge was annoyed—for only a moment—and then he realized and rolled over on his back and let the rain pour into his face, his eyes, run into his mouth. He funnelled his hands beside his mouth and brushed the droplets past his lips. He delighted in the taste. The water couldn't come down fast enough for him. He almost let himself laugh out loud. The water was cascading over the rocks around him, running in streams, creating a small waterfall that dropped into the pool below.

He looked down to the Drac. It had leapt to its feet. It was standing there, face turned to the sky, mouth open to catch the falling water, arms wide in benediction. Abruptly, it dove into the lagoon, swimming powerfully beneath the rain-splattering surface.

Davidge stared. Was this his chance? Could he make it to the capsule? If only the Drac would stay under the water. If only—

Davidge leapt to his feet and scrambled *up* the slope, over the rocks and down again to the wreckage of the Drac marauder, his body bent forward against the wind and the driving rain. He slid, scrambled down the last few feet to the intact section of the marauder's hull and began to pull at the tank mountings.

8

UNDER THE SURFACE OF THE WATER, there was silence. The Drac twisted and turned among the rocks with the lethal grace of a shark. Its yellow eyes were wide and expressionless.

It came up once, floating soundlessly in the water, turning and looking, surveying the shore of the lagoon and the capsule, and then it noiselessly sank back under the surface of the black water again.

It dove down deep, luxuriating in the freedom, winding its way carefully across the bottom of the pool.

Had the Drac looked up, it would have seen a pale mauve liquid spreading out across the surface of the water.

But nothing else.

Davidge was hidden. He stood on the rocks above, pouring the bubbling, hissing oil into the streaming water that arced out over the edge of the rocks and into the pool below. The glistening fuel was a layer of darkness on dark.

When the fuel pod was empty Davidge tossed it aside. He pulled a distress flare from the leg of his flight suit, took a half step forward, leaning to see that the shadowy figure of the Drac was still beneath the water, and then fired the flare directly into the lagoon below.

With a noise like the fist of God, the rocket fuel ignited! A wall of flame tore across the surface of the lagoon. Oily black smoke poured upward into the sky, illuminated by the orange glare of the flames below.

Davidge didn't wait. Shielding his face against the intense heat, he hurled himself down the steep slope toward the capsule.

Something was splashing and hissing in the water— Davidge didn't turn to look. He didn't want to see. The goddamn lizard deserved it.

And then, with a chilling roar, something burst out of the lagoon, out of flames in front of him! The Drac, eyes blazing, stood there—somehow miraculously escaped—at the edge of the inferno.

Davidge opened his mouth in horror. "Oh, shit," he said.

The Drac said nothing. Oil and water dripped from its skin. Was it too stunned to realize?

Davidge dashed for the capsule, his feet plowing desperately against the soft sand. The Drac made no attempt to stop him. It simply watched silently.

Davidge stopped at the hatch and looked back. The Drac still hadn't moved.

"Hah! You blew it, Toadface!"

He grabbed the rifle and stiffened as if he'd been kicked. Every muscle in his body contracted instantly! The world was crackling and arcing with blue sparks! The goddamn lizard had hot-wired the rifle! The agony was numbing.

The Drac walked slowly toward the spasming Davidge and kicked his hand off the rifle. Davidge slumped forward onto his face, his knees drawn up to his chest, still twitching in reaction and shock.

The Drac looked down at the contorted human and said, *"Gon bidden, Irkmann."*

9

THE DRAC WAS EATING AGAIN—a long, yellow thing that was either a pickled root or some kind of fish. It dripped with a slimy white sauce. The Drac seemed to like it. It bit and chewed and smacked its lips. The process would have been fascinating, if it weren't so angering.

Good lord! How much food did the damn creature need? More important, just how much food was there stashed in that capsule?

Davidge couldn't take his eyes off the food.

He was tied and bound, his hands lashed behind his back and tied to the capsule. His feet were also tied together. But it was the pain in his stomach that commanded his attention.

"Hey!"

The Drac glanced over at him, a quick, contemptuous glance, then returned to its lip-smacking.

"*Hey!* I'm hungry! Can you understand that? Hungry! HUNGRY!" Davidge opened his mouth wide, like a gaping baby bird, hoping to convey the idea of hunger.

The Drac looked at this gesture for a moment, then opened its mouth wide also. It held this grimace for a long taunting moment, then continued eating.

Davidge's rage pounded in his head. *"Hey! You understand any English, Toadface?!!"* he bellowed as loud as he could. For a moment it blanked out the pain and hunger.

The Drac leapt to its feet, almost dropping the food. It came rushing up to Davidge—he cringed in reaction— but the Drac stopped two feet short of him and pointed a long, clawed finger at the Earthman's face.

"Kos son va?"

"What?"

"Kos son va?"

"Stick it."

The Drac seemed annoyed, irritated. It tried again. *"Ohy! Ohy! Kos son va?"* It turned the pointing finger at itself. *"Kos va son Jeriba Shigan. Shhhigan!"*

Davidge blinked, and understood. "So you're Jerry Shigan. I'm really impressed."

"Ae! Te gavey! Bini, bini, bini. Kos son va, Irk-mann?"

"You want to know my name? Davidge, Willis E. Also known as Willy. Willis E. Davidge. Now how about some food? Food!"

"Ae! Shigan gavey. Irkmann hotetsa yida. Foood!" The Drac smirked and uttered a hissing sound, a lizard laugh.

It turned and walked away from the capsule and picked up a stick from the pile next to the campfire. It strode down toward the water's edge and speared a large, pink slug. It came back, carrying the slug at arm's length and held it in front of Davidge's face.

"Na, Davidge. Vot fooood! Et yida, eh?"

"You're kidding."

"Ae! Ae! Ae! Kiiddiing! Vot yida—food!"

Davidge looked at the pulsating slug before him. Part of his mind was recoiling in horror—but his body was aching so badly! Before he could stop himself, he stretched his neck, shut his eyes and gobbled the slimy thing off the stick.

The Drac recoiled, staring at him in utter horror and disbelief. The joke suddenly had turned very sour. *"Gefh! Gefh!"*

It turned and walked back to its place by the campfire. It sat down and picked up its survival food, looked at it, then put it down again. It was too disgusted to eat.

━━━━━10

THE CAMPFIRE BURNED LOW. Soft blue flames flickered over the embers. The damp wood crackled and hissed and spat. The Drac lay curled up on the warm sand beside it, sleeping as soundly as a cat.

Davidge was still tied up. His shoulders ached like liquid fire. His back was stiff and hurting, his spine felt like it was hardening into stone. And his gut was twisting and turning, in pain, unable to decide if it should reject the slug by nausea or diarrhea. Davidge felt as if he was going to lose control at both ends. And if that weren't enough discomfort, somehow he had gotten sand in his shorts. It was driving him crazy.

His wrists were raw too. He'd been working at his bonds for hours, trying to loosen them, trying to wear a weak spot in the cords, but all he'd succeeded in doing was chafing the skin on his wrists until they were red and scraped.

Something moved across the distant sky—a streak of fire.

Davidge sat up straighter. Sharp pains leapt up his spine, he almost gasped aloud but he sat up straighter and squinted into the distance. *They're looking for me!*

And then the streak of fire swelled and flared and burnt itself out in the atmosphere.

It had only been a meteor.

Davidge slumped in disappointment.

A second, brighter meteor streaked across the sky. And then a third one, bigger and closer than the other two. It flickered and flared—a blue core with streaming orange flames spreading out around it—and disappeared into darkness. A fourth meteor crossed the sky in the distance. And then a fifth and a sixth, and—

Suddenly, there were too many to count. The entire sky was ablaze with lights, long chains of sparks, rosettes of flame, flashing and exploding like fireworks only brighter and wilder.

Something as tiny as a firefly flashed past Davidge's face, stinging the sand and popping like a firecracker— and leaving a soup-bowl sized crater.

"What the hell?"

A second explosion of sand scoured his eyes and face! Davidge looked around in abrupt terror. The surface of the lagoon was exploding with spouts of water shooting violently upward.

"Drac! Wake up!"

There was no response. The Drac slumbered on.

"Hey, Drac! WAKE UP!"

A meteor exploded into the rocks above, sparking a shower of stinging rocks and sand. Davidge ducked his head. The Drac still slept on.

Davidge started struggling against his bonds. "Come on, Toadface!"

The sand exploded just in front of the Drac's face, a sudden stinging gout of dirt. The Drac sat up with a bark, its eyes angry and glaring.

"It's a meteor shower! We're in the middle of a meteor shower!"

The Drac was already turning and looking in wonderment and fear. The sky was on fire. Shooting stars drove across the night with a dreadful roar. The horizon all around them was a flashing horror.

"Zeerki!" screamed the Drac.

"Yeah, *zeerki!"* Davidge continued to work at his bonds.

The Drac leapt to its feet and ran for the overhang of the rocky escarpment.

"Hey!" Davidge shouted. "Drac! Help me!"

The Drac paused. The sand exploded at its feet. It leapt backward, startled, then dashed back toward Davidge. Wielding its own knife, it cut the wires binding Davidge's legs, then pulled him up and pushed him roughly toward the rocks. Davidge ran as best he could.

The two of them, lizard and human, scrambled across the spattering sand. The Drac dove into a cleft in the rock, pulling Davidge in after. Hot rocks stung their backs. They fell inward, lying side-by-side, both gasping for breath, while the rocks around them popped with the impact of tiny meteorites. Something went *bang* uncomfortably close, spraying them both with slivers of burning stone.

"Kiz! Ox da kiz!"

"You said it!" grunted Davidge. "Definitely *ox da kiz."* He was suddenly uncomfortably aware how close he was to the lizard. They were as close as lovers. He could smell the Drac's hot breath. It wasn't as bad as he would have thought. In fact, the Drac didn't smell bad at all. Kind of dry and sweet and musky all at once.

He let himself look into the Drac's face, really *look.* The Drac's wide yellow eyes were peering back into his. The Drac's expression was emotionless.

What is it thinking? Davidge wondered. *If it were going to kill me, it wouldn't have saved me.*

It didn't make sense.

11

DAVIDGE AWOKE WITH A START—and realized abruptly where he was.

He had slept with a lizard. Next to a lizard. A stinking, goddamn lizard. The Drac was still asleep; its breathing was a gentle hissing *susurrus*.

Davidge didn't move. He didn't want to alarm the Drac—or wake it. He had to think. His knife, where was it? The last time he had seen it, the Drac had... been putting it into its belt. Davidge eased his hands downward, easing the knife out of the Drac's belt, opened it, turned and wedged it into a rock, then carefully, slowly, laboriously began to saw at the bonds around his wrists. They parted abruptly and his hands were free again.

He grabbed the knife from the rock and turned back to the lizard, bringing the point of the blade toward the sleeping Drac's throat.

And then he stopped.

He couldn't do it.

It would be... dishonorable.

Damn it.

Instead, Davidge closed his knife and edged quietly out of the cleft. He straightened up in the bright glare of the gray morning, blinking and rubbing his eyes.

The capsule. Food!

He headed across the sand. His body ached; he lumbered painfully—but the capsule stood open. The sand around it was dotted with tiny craters from last night's meteor shower. His mouth was already watering in anticipation.

Davidge moved around the capsule gingerly. He could still feel the electrical kick of the Drac's last booby trap. His elbows twinged at the memory. Finally, Davidge reached forward, reached into the capsule, careful not to touch the metal hull or the door frame.

His fingers closed around a ration bar; he brought it out into the glare of day. The wrapping felt strange, looked unpleasant. He sniffed at it. It had no smell. Fumbling, he opened his knife again and slit open the wrapping.

It was a root of some kind. Pickled. Yellow. Slimy. Davidge paused, trying to prepare his stomach. It wouldn't work. He was just going to have to do it, once and for all. *You can do it,* he told himself. *After all, you ate the slug.* The memory didn't help.

Davidge squeezed a little bit of the ration bar out of the wrapper. He bit, chewed, tried desperately not to taste what was happening, and swallowed quickly.

Despite his attempt to keep his tongue from knowing what the rest of his mouth was doing, he still found himself tasting the root as it slid past. It was . . . it was . . . disgusting.

Absolutely disgusting.

It was like eating someone's infection.

It felt like the inside of a jellyfish and tasted like— he didn't want to think what it tasted like. He forced himself to take another bite.

Suddenly something swept his feet out from under him and he was sprawling flat on the sand. Davidge rolled and came up with his knife at the ready, but the Drac had its rifle pointed at his face.

"Listen, Drac. I could have killed you easy, back there."

He nodded toward the cave. "I took my knife. I could have killed you." He held up the knife and gestured. The Drac's eyes were unblinking. The rifle was unwavering. "You owe me one."

The Drac blinked slowly, but it didn't move. What was it thinking? That was the trouble with the goddamned lizards. You couldn't read their expressions.

"You owe me one," he repeated. He put his knife aside and picked up the ration bar again and squeezed a little bit more out of the wrapper and bit it off. He tried hard not to grimace. Maybe, if you ate enough of this stuff, you could get used to it. He took another bite. And another. He was wrong. The taste was relentless. Nobody could get used to this. He ate anyway, finishing the bar as quickly as he could.

The Drac watched his every movement. It looked tense. Worried.

"What did you say your name was?" He pointed at the Drac. "Name. Your name?"

"Kos? Jeriba Shigan."

"All right, Jerry. Now listen..." He paused. How could he explain? This was a lizard! He'd have to pantomime the whole thing. He took a breath. "Meteors. Meteors fall here. Many meteors fall. You *gavey?*"

"Ohy," said the Drac. *"Yan ohyn gavey. Ova* meteors?"

That sounded like no. No, I don't understand. What are meteors?

Davidge frowned. What was it the Drac had said last night? Zeerki? *"Zeerki?"* he said. "Meteors. *Zeerki. Zeerki?* Is that right? *Zeerki?* Meteors."

"Ae! Gavey. Zeerki." The Drac nodded. Nodded? Davidge stared, surprised at seeing such a human gesture.

"Okay. Good. *Zeerki* fall here. We're in the open." He pantomimed falling *zeerki.* He pantomimed *zeerki*

falling on his head, falling on the Drac's head. He opened
his hands and spread them wide. "This is too . . . open.
Too unprotected. If we stay down here, we die." He
made a face and fell over backward to indicate death.
Did the Drac understand? He felt like an idiot. He sat
up again. *"Gavey?"*

"Nekhem-Biekhem. Die."

"Yeah. You got it. I think. Why don't we take . . ."
He pantomimed picking up and carrying. "Why don't
we take all the goodies out of that thing of yours . . ."
He pointed at the capsule.

"Naesay," said the Drac.

"Yeah, from that *naesay* and get our butts up higher,
into the forest. At least there's some cover there." He
pointed and gestured and danced, pantomiming carrying
an invisible load from the *naesay* up to the higher ground.
The Drac watched without expression.

When Davidge finished he turned to Jeriba Shigan
and waited for a reaction.

Jeriba Shigan lowered its rifle and said, *"Irkmann, ta
govert ymno, me sto ya verit ta, eh? Ta tolki vyezhdi,
neb ya derzho rozzo."*

Davidge didn't understand a word of it.

But the meaning was clear. Yes, let's do it.

Davidge grinned. "Terrific! I thought it was a good
idea myself!"

══════ 12

DAVIDGE WAS EXHAUSTED. He sank to his knees gasping. He hadn't realized how hard this was going to be. They'd piled as much of the rations as they could into sacks of parachute silk, slung the sacks over their backs and begun struggling over the rocks and up the slope toward the distant trees.

"Wait," he panted, holding up a hand, "let me catch my breath." It was the strain. He knew it, two days without food and then nothing to eat but a pink slug and a ration of slime. It was too much to ask of a human body and then expect it to perform strenuous labor.

The Drac was laughing at him. It was hissing and wearing that peculiar smirk—the closest thing to an expression that a lizard could have. It stood balancing its heavy pack easily.

"Fmlk you," Davidge mumbled and staggered back to his feet. Maybe he would kill the lizard after all.

Somehow, they made it to the forest.

Davidge thought of it as the Dead Forest.

The old gnarled trees were blackened and scarred; they looked burnt. The branches twisted upwards, bending and turning like claws. Purplish vines wrapped around the trunks and branches. Sheets of blue moss hung from above, looking like tattered veils. The floor of the forest was a damp carpet of decaying leaves, rustling in the brooding wind. What daylight there was, filtered through the branches in gloomy dust-laden streaks. It smelled dry and musty.

They walked slowly, picking their way over half-buried roots and boulders, avoiding the gnarly bushes and the occasional cracks and rills in the earth. Often, they had to stop and rest. Davidge had to stop and rest—the Drac would wait. Davidge ignored its constant hissing and smirking. He didn't care.

He plodded on. He lost track of the time and followed. Sometimes he pointed, remembering a landmark or a direction. They climbed up through the sloping forest. Davidge faded in and out of awareness, letting his legs move of their own accord, letting his feet pick their own way—until he came down on something hard that twisted out from under his foot and he almost sprawled flat on his face. He caught himself, jerked awake and realized that he had been walking blindly after the Drac for so long, he didn't know where he was anymore. He'd been sleepwalking for the last fifteen minutes.

He stopped and looked around.

They were in a flat area, a clearing in the Dead Forest. There were rocks and boulders scattered around like the ruins of an ancient temple. Worst of all, the place smelled like death, a sickly-sweet rotting odor, though Davidge couldn't see what was causing it. Maybe the tattered blue veils of moss. There were fallen branches here too—limbs broken from the trees by the meteor showers. It was one of these that Davidge had almost tripped over.

A clearing?

This clearing would work. It would have to work. His knees suddenly buckled—

"This is it!" Davidge gasped, dropping his sack. "I can't go another step." The sack split open on the ground, spilling its contents: ration bars, wires, other odds and ends salvaged from the *naesay*.

The Drac turned angrily, raising its rifle and pressing the barrel up against Davidge's head.

Davidge was too exhausted to be scared. He said, "Okay Toadface, you want to shoot me so bad? Go ahead. Shoot me. Now. Do it now!"

The Drac wavered uncertainly.

"—'Cause the question is, Draco, whether *we* live or die. I don't love you, and you don't love me. But we're stranded here, buddy. Stuck, abandoned . . . marooned! Get it? Or don't you *gavey* Engl-eeeeesh?"

The Drac looked at him sullenly, but it lowered the rifle. When it spoke, there was anger in its voice. *"Irkmann! Ta aba pravo. May ta ib phtuga! Phtuga!"*

"Yeah, yeah. Write and tell my mother." He stared defiantly at the Drac. The Drac's yellow eyes were impossible to read. The hell with it.

Davidge squatted down and picked up one of the brick-sized boulders littering the ground. The Drac tensed—

"You're too fucking paranoid," Davidge muttered. He grabbed another rock and put the two of them together. "What we need to do is build a shelter, *gavey*? A shelter with stones." Oh, God. Was he going to have to pantomime the whole construction?

The Drac stared at him for a moment longer then turned and leaned its rifle up against a tree, lowered its sack to the ground and began to gather up rocks.

"Well, I'll be damned," said Davidge.

"Phtuga!" said Jeriba Shigan.

13

THE SHELTER BEGAN as a circular foundation of stones. Shigan gathered them from the area around the clearing and Davidge laid them out carefully.

The work was slow going. Davidge kept his mind occupied by learning to speak Drac. He turned the words and phrases over in his mind, stringing them together into rudimentary sentences. And then he tried them out on Jerry Shigan.

"Hey Drac," Davidge called. Shigan was just entering the clearing, carrying a head-sized boulder. The Drac put the boulder down and looked at Davidge curiously.

Davidge said carefully, *"Ya navo . . . nuvo . . . tut . . . toot . . . tutas—"*

The Drac was staring at him in total incomprehension.

"Never mind, forget it." Davidge waved his hands in the air as if to erase what he had said. "Sorry."

The Drag shrugged—a gesture it had learned from Davidge—and turned away to get another stone.

"I wonder what I said," Davidge muttered, and continued mixing up a mortar of mud and clay and vine fibers. "I gotta watch myself, or I might say something really stupid."

The walls of the shelter grew a little bit higher every day. And Davidge learned a little bit more of the Drac language every day as well.

The Drac was also learning English.

"Shit!" it said.

"Huh?" asked Davidge, turning to Shigan. "What are you talking about?"

"No solid," said the Drac, pointing at the nearly-finished shelter. It shook its head.

"Not solid?!!" Davidge was angered at the Drac's opinion. "No solid. Watch this." He picked up the largest boulder he could and gave it a mighty heave against the rock wall of the shelter.

The boulder bounced harmlessly off and fell to the ground with a soft *thud*.

The shelter stood unharmed.

Davidge turned to grin at Shigan—

—and then *spang*, a very small rock popped off the top of the shelter. And then another and another, and suddenly the whole structure was cascading downward and outward in a small furious avalanche.

Jerry Shigan turned to Willy Davidge, smiled, hissed and said, "Shit." The Drac was proud to be right.

"I don't know what you're so happy about," said Davidge sadly. "This just means another night sleeping outside on the cold ground."

The Drac blinked. It stopped laughing. After a moment, it said, "Is sorry, Willy."

Now it was Davidge's turn to look startled.

Shigan added, "Is wrong. Is hurt. Is hurt shared. So is wrong—wrong joy. *Te guvo foy*—" Abruptly, it stopped itself, shaking its head. The phrase wouldn't translate.

Davidge turned and looked at the scattered pile of rocks. He scratched his head. "I suppose we could try again."

14

THEY FOUND A HOLLOW TREE TRUNK INSTEAD.

It wasn't much, but it was shelter of a sort. It gave them some small protection against the wind and perhaps might even give them some protection against the next night of meteors. Maybe they could find a cave.

There was wood, plenty of it, and it burned with a spicy, not unpleasant smell, so they had fire. At least they were warm and that was something.

Davidge sat close to the campfire, warming his hands and feet. He couldn't say he felt good, but he didn't hurt as much as he had. That was something too.

And his stomach didn't hurt tonight. That was another thing to feel good about.

And he was alive and he wasn't alone. His companion was only a lizard, a goddamn lizard, but at least he had something to talk to.

Jerry Shigan was pointing and reciting, "This. Is. My. Right. Foot. This. Is. My. Left. Foot. These. Are. Both. My. Feet."

Davidge yawned. "Fine. Great."

Shigan hissed and smiled, obviously pleased. "Great. Yeah. Great!" The Drac pointed to its head. "And. This. Is. My. Head."

Davidge reached up and caught its hand. "No. That's your *ugly* head."

Shigan nodded enthusiastically. "Yeah. Great. This.

45

Is. My. *Ugly*. Head." The Drac repeated. "My. Ugly. Head." Shigan looked to Davidge for approval. "Is right? Right?"

Davidge felt like a worm. Like a pink slug. He looked at Shigan's bright eyes and sighed. "No. Is wrong. I am sorry. Shigan is not ugly."

"Not. Ugly?"

"Not."

Shigan looked puzzled. "Is can't be ugly?"

"Is bad joke," Davidge said. "Damn! Now you've got me talking that way. Ugly is..." Davidge pondered for an instant, then made a face, sticking out his tongue and grimacing horribly. "Ugly is *Yicchh!*" He looked to Shigan. "Shigan is not ugly. Shigan is not *Yicchh!* I played a joke. Bad joke."

"Bad joke?"

"Not funny. I'm sorry."

Shigan studied Davidge for a moment, then nodded thoughtfully. *"Te gavey."*

They were both silent for a moment.

The Drac spoke first. "Is...?" it began, then frowned. It didn't know the English word. It held up a single clawed finger, as if to ask a question. "What is word for good...good speak? No, not good speak. Good inside..." It frowned. It pointed to itself. "Drac good inside. Is called *shizza.*"

"Shizza. Right." Davidge considered the thought. Was Shigan talking about honor? Integrity? He hadn't realized that the Dracs had any—but of course they would have to, wouldn't they? He wasn't happy with the thought. It didn't fit in with the rest of his pictures. Either it was wrong, or the pictures were—he put that thought aside. Honor. It had to be honor. He looked at Shigan and said, "Is honor. When a human has good inside, we say, he has honor."

"Honor! Good!" Shigan pointed at Davidge. "Davidge has honor."

Davidge was startled. "What? Why do you say that, Drac?"

"Is . . ." Shigan frowned. "How to explain? Hard. Davidge say bad joke. Davidge clean up bad joke. Bad joke not more bad. Davidge not laugh at Drac not know. *Te gavey?*"

"Te gavey." Davidge added, "But, that's not really honor, Jerry."

"Not?"

"Well, maybe it is. I guess it is, after all. But I always thought . . . I mean, it's just something I learned as a kid."

"Kid?"

"Umm, hatchling? Baby?" Davidge pantomimed a small person in his arms. "Small person?"

"Ae. Te gavey."

"Good. When I was a small person, I was taught . . . umm, how to say it? Don't do to someone anything . . . got that? . . . anything that you wouldn't want them to do to you."

Shigan frowned oddly. Davidge had never seen that expression on the lizard's face before. "Is say again, please?"

Davidge repeated it. "Don't do anything to another person that you wouldn't want them to do to you. *Ta gavey?*"

"Te gavey," said Shigan, then spoke again with sudden intensity, *"Irkmann!* Is humans study *Shizumaat?"*

"Is humans study—what? What is *Shizumaat?"*

"What is—?" Shigan looked startled and offended; then softened and said, *"Shizumaat* is . . . is great Drac . . ." The Drac stopped and frowned, looking for a word. "Teacher!"

"Oh," said Davidge. *Shizumaat* was a teacher. Or

maybe something more. He hadn't taught Shigan the words for prophet or messiah. He wasn't sure he ought to. That might open up the whole question of souls— and who had one and who didn't.

Shigan asked again. "Is not learn this lesson from *Shizumaat*, then who—?"

Davidge grinned, remembering. The first time he had heard the golden rule had been—he almost laughed out loud. "Is learned from great Earth teacher."

"Be name?"

"Mickey Mouse."

"Mickey Mooze? Is great *Irkmann* teacher?"

Davidge nodded, still grinning. "Yeah. Sort of." Then he added, "If you're good, someday I'll even tell you about Bugs Bunny." He scratched his head. "I should have listened to him better. If I had I wouldn't be here. I'd have turned left at Albuquerque."

Shigan was frowning. "Is not follow."

Davidge waved it away. "Don't worry about it, Jerry. Is another bad joke—stupid joke."

And then he had to explain to Shigan the difference between bad jokes and dumb jokes. It took the better part of an hour.

Davidge's last thought before he fell asleep that night was this: *I hope to God I never make the mistake of telling him about the leprechauns and the penguin. I'll never be able to explain about* dirty *jokes!*

15

THE DRAC RATIONS WEREN'T GOING TO LAST FOREVER.

Davidge knew it. They were going to have to find something else to eat. And soon.

He wondered about the pink slugs. The one he'd eaten hadn't made him too sick. Maybe there was some way they could be prepared or cooked? After all, he'd learned to like *escargot*—well, tolerate them anyway.

It was worth an experiment at least.

By the time his beard had completely darkened the lower part of his face he'd found a way to eat the pink slugs. They were almost—no, not tasty. Never *tasty*. But they were *tolerable*. Given enough time— He thrust the thought away in disgust. He didn't want to consider that he might be here on this planet long enough to start relishing the taste of the slugs.

No, the more he thought about it, the more he was certain he'd never be able to get the *ug* out of slug. He'd have to share that joke with Jerry. Maybe Jerry would get it. Maybe not. Either way, it would be something to talk about and that would lead to something else to talk about. It didn't matter what they talked about as long as they were talking. It was better than being alone with his thoughts.

He was striding through the forest carrying a bundle of parts salvaged from the wreck of his escape pod— tubes of various lengths, chunks of metal, pieces of fuselage, sharp slivers of glass that could be used as knives, bits of wire, a tool kit, anything that he could find that might conceivably be useful.

Rak-a-tak-a-tak.

Davidge froze.

Rak-a-tak-a-tak.

There was something scurrying through the roots of the trees he called Grandfather Banyans. The roots were thick and curled along the ground like serpents.

Rak-a-tak-a-tak.

Davidge dropped his bundle to the ground and edged forward, curiously. The scurrying thing looked like a turtle with a pig snout. Two snouts. It was dog-sized and it sniffed and snorfled its way through the roots, tapping at them and making a noise in its throat:

Rak-a-tak-a-tak.

Davidge watched it, grinning; his eyes were shining. Now there was something to tell Shigan about. Another new creature. He wondered if it was edible? He could call it a Mock Turtle, and then, of course, he'd have to explain about Alice in Wonderland. Did the Dracs have a fantasy equivalent, he wondered?

He picked up his bundle and sauntered on. That was something to think about. Did the Dracs even have imagination? He couldn't imagine that they did, but on the other hand, Jerry had raised the question of honor. Could a species be honorable without being able to envision honor?

What was Drac honor like anyway? Hmm. He'd have to ask Jerry more about that. The last time they'd tried to talk about it, they didn't have enough words. The best that Jerry could say was, "Is no bad. Is no good. Bad–good is only life-opinion. Universe not care if bad–good. Only life care. Honor come when life look beyond itself.

Beyond—survival." An interesting thought that one; it kept ricocheting around Davidge's consciousness like an elusive butterfly. Well, maybe *Shizumaat* could explain it better. He'd ask Jerry about it after dinner.

Dinner was pink slugs wrapped in purple vine-leaves. He spitted them on a long stick and roasted them over the fire like marshmallows. The purple vine-leaves were like grape leaves or spinach or cabbage, depending on how young they were. They gave the slugs a spicy taste, neither bad nor good but closer to tolerable. Within that range of closer-to-tolerable, Davidge could at least begin to appreciate his newly-developing skill as a chef. Well, maybe not a chef, but definitely some sort of culinary camouflage artist.

At least it was better than the Drac slime that Jerry called food. Even the scent of those could be overpowering. He insisted that Jerry stay downwind when he ate. The Drac responded by taking most of its meals privately. When Davidge ate, Shigan retreated into the pages of the *Talman*, a tiny golden book that it wore on a chain around its neck. The Drac made a point of ignoring Davidge's meals.

And Davidge made a point of teasing the Drac about it whenever he could.

Tonight, for instance. Davidge took a bite of slug, then still chewing, offered the shish-ka-bob skewer to Shigan. "Delicious. Mmmmm." He rubbed his stomach. "Try one, Jerry?"

Shigan looked at him, eyes round with disgust, then turned away pointedly.

"Hey, don't forget who helped me acquire the taste." Davidge grinned and took another bite. He chewed as loudly as he could and with as much gusto as he could pretend. Roasted, the slugs took on the texture of crunchy hardboiled eggs. The taste, however, was still the same. Davidge crunched louder.

The Drac cringed.

"Besides, I'm going to improve the menu for both of us," Davidge added;

"Your bow and arrow is too crude, *Irkmann*. We starve first."

"I'll get better. Rome wasn't built in a day, you know."

"Is not matter. Soon we picked up. One side or other side." The Drac's tone was sullen.

Davidge considered the thought, then shook his head. "Not with this war going. I just don't see it."

"Humans!" The Drac spat on the ground in front of itself. "Easy you give up. Argue always for limits. *Shizumaat* say..." Shigan paused and frowned, searching for the words. "*Shizumaat* say, 'Intelligent life... takes a stand.'"

"Give me a break, will you." Davidge said, annoyed. "I am taking a stand! I'm taking a stand on the whole goddamn planet! I'm the one with all the ideas! Without me, where the hell would you be? And just remember, neither of us would be here tonight if it weren't for you sons of *Shizumaat!*"

"*Shiz-u-maat*," Shigan corrected carefully.

"Yeah, whatever!"

"And this war. It begun by you. By humans."

"Huh? Did *Shiz-u-maat*—" Davidge was deliberately overcareful with the pronunciation, "—did *Shiz-u-maat* say that too?"

The Drac made a noise, a high-pitched whistling hiss, that Davidge had learned to recognize as annoyance. He called it the Oliver Hardy whistle. Shigan made the noise whenever it considered some remark of Davidge's too stupid to be worthy of a reply.

"Yeah, same to you fella. And *Shizumaat* too." Just

for good measure, he added, *"Shizumaat* eats the *kiz* of scavenger pigs!"

Shigan turned around, horrified. The Drac's eyes were wider than Davidge had ever seen them before. This reaction went beyond anger. Its expression was livid. Two air bladders on either side of its face were puffing up in rage.

Davidge tensed. Had he gone too far?

Shigan took three quick breaths and suddenly spat, *"Irkmann,* your Mickey Mooze is one big, stupid dope!"

Davidge stared, astonished. The laughter came bulging up his throat in one painful hiccup; he clenched his teeth, trying to stifle it, puffed his cheeks rather than let the air escape, the mounting pressure sprayed bits of food across the campfire. Davidge felt his eyes watering, his throat constricting; somehow he turned the feelings into a ghastly choking fit instead. He didn't dare let on—

Somehow he brought himself under control, pounding himself on his chest with one fist. Somehow he kept his face straight. He looked over at Shigan. The Drac's air sacs had gone down, but it still looked sullen and hurt.

Davidge felt ashamed.

Should he apologize?

He didn't know. Maybe . . . maybe it would be best to just forget the moment and move beyond it. He turned away, looking for something to be busy with. He came up with his bow and arrow; he stood up, hooked one foot against one end of the bow, bent it backward and strung it. He tested the tautness of the line with one finger. It was as rigid as if it were made out of metal. Good. He notched an arrow and took aim at a distant tree—*fffwwsssst!*

The arrow flew clean and straight, imbedding itself with a loud *Thwock!* into the trunk of the tree.

"Ha!" he exclaimed. "Look at that."

The Drac turned slowly and looked.

"See? Jerry, old Drac, where would you be without me?"

The Drac didn't answer. It just turned back to its study of the *Talman*.

═══════ 16

DAVIDGE DISCOVERED QUICKLY that he could approach the Mock Turtles quite closely before they would scurry off into the roots of the Grandfather Banyans. They seemed to have no fear; either they were too stupid or there were no predators of significant size that could menace a Mock Turtle.

Davidge wasn't so stupid as to assume the former. The tendency of life was to grow as large as it could. If there was prey, there were predators. If it moved, it was prey. If not for something else, then for Davidge.

He took aim carefully. The arrows weren't hard to make, but it was slow tedious work. Every shot had to count. The fat little turtle-pig was tapping its way slowly along the roots of the tree, looking for insects and grubs. Davidge licked his lips and sighted. "Come to Poppa, little lunch."

The creature hesitated on the branch, its two pig-snouts probing—

Davidge released the arrow—

—it buried itself in the creature's body, right between two shell segments. The Mock Turtle shrieked, spasmed, rolled, tried to run, spasmed again and collapsed in a limp heap on the edge of a sandy depression.

"Son of a bitch," said Davidge, standing up. "It worked! It actually worked! Hah!" He ran over to the Mock Turtle and began to dance a little jig of joy around the creature's body. "Hah! Hah! That'll show you, Jerry Shigan, you Drac doubting Thomas!"

He stopped then and began to wonder how he was going to carry the creature home. He could probably heave it onto his shoulders—if he could get a grip on it. He circled the animal thoughtfully—

One foot skidded onto the edge of the sand pit—skidded and slipped—he was tumbling. The sand was like grease under his feet. He skidded a short way into the pit. He tried to climb out, but this only triggered new waves of sand shimmering down the sides. He redoubled his efforts, falling to his hands and knees and scrambling—

It was then that he noticed the scattering of bones, small skulls and shells around the edge of the pit.

"Uh oh. . . ."

The sand at the center of the pit was beginning to stir.

"Oh, sweet Jesus." The fear came rising up in Davidge like a cork released at fifty fathoms. He flattened himself on the sand and began to breast stroke upward and outward. It almost worked. It would have worked—if the thing at the bottom of the pit hadn't started pulling the sand out from under Davidge's feet. He started sliding backward—

A long, pink vine came sliding up from the center of the sand pit, waving gently.

"Ohhh, shit—" Davidge froze. Maybe if he held perfectly still, it couldn't locate him.

The vine hesitated. Then it began wavering again.

It might work, for a while. But sooner or later, the thing would find him. Davidge began to scream, "Jerrrrrrryyyyy!!!"

The vine trembled, aroused. It began poking the sand, blindly. It moved as if it were searching.

"Jerrrrrryyyyyy!! Heeellllpp!!"

The pink vine poked, poked again. It raised up, hesitating. It had never encountered anything like this before. It rested one end on the sand.

Davidge, looking back, held absolutely still. The vine-thing was tracking the vibrations—movement or screaming, it didn't matter. The vine lifted—

"Jeeerrrrrryyyyyy!!!! Heeelllppp! Heeelllppp Meeee!!! Oh, come on, please! You goddamn lizard!"

The vine vibrated angrily. It swayed and circled and dropped within inches of his horrified face. He froze. The vine hesitated—

Through the trees, he could see something moving— Jerry! The Drac was searching for him. He was starting to turn away— "Jeerrryyyy! Over here!"

The Drac turned—Davidge threw himself sideways— and the pink vine snapped whip-like around his leg. It constricted and started pulling—the pain in his leg was fiery. The sand around him started sliding. Davidge flailed—a three-fingered hand grabbed his.

The Drac was lying flat on the sand, using its own weight to oppose the tugging of the vine. With its other hand it steadied its rifle. Davidge was screaming with the pain now. The Drac fired!

The ground shook and roared—and then a pink, hairless head came thrusting up through the sand at the center of the pit. It was a long head with a mouth full of jagged teeth. The pink vine—now half blown away—was the creature's tongue, still protruding from its gigantic mouth, now flailing back and forth in burning agony. High on the creature's head, two blood-red eyes glared at them.

Jerry fired again! The fleshy part of the monster's head splattered away. A long sighing noise came issuing from its throat—its smell was terrible—and then the creature began sinking slowly back into its hole.

The Drac held the rifle steady for a moment longer.

Only after it was certain that the creature was truly dead did it begin pulling Davidge out of the sand to firmer ground.

For a moment, the two of them just lay on the dirt, gasping and looking at each other. Davidge caught his breath first and managed a quiet, "Thank you, Jerry. Thank you for saving my life."

17

DAVIDGE'S LEG WAS BURNING UP. The sand pit monster must have had a poisonous tongue. He could barely stand. He had to lean on Jerry all the way back to the camp.

"I ruined my surprise." Davidge pointed weakly at the Mock Turtle carcass.

Jerry hissed. "I am surprised enough for one day, thank you, Willy." But the Drac stopped long enough to admire Davidge's marksmanship. "One shot?"

"Yeah," Davidge grinned. "Disgusting, isn't it?"

"Amazing," corrected the Drac. He resumed the burden of Davidge's weight, and they continued staggering back toward camp. "I will come back for it. First, I must . . ." Jerry looked at Davidge with a peculiar expression. *"Irkmann,* can you trust a goddamn lizard?"

"Huh?" Davidge looked startled. *I never taught him that phrase. Do the Dracs read minds as well? Or do I talk in my sleep?*

"Well, can you?" The Drac asked again.

Davidge shrugged. "I don't really have much of a choice, do I? You're already carrying me home. What are you trying not to say, Drac?"

"Your leg. The wound. It must be . . . burned. To avoid illness."

"Oh, shit. You're right." Davidge didn't speak for a moment.

"Can you trust a goddamn lizard, *Irkmann?"*

Davidge almost didn't hear the question this time—
he was still trying not to think about his leg. The pain.
The wound. Cauterization. No anaesthetics. No matter
how bad he imagined it was going to be, it would be
worse.

"Huh? Don't be silly, Drac." He said it in a preoc-
cupied tone. "You saved my life. Of course, I trust you."

"Is good."

They arrived at their camp then. The Drac lowered
Davidge carefully to the ground, leaning him up against
the hollow tree trunk, then turned to the smouldering
campfire and began stirring up the embers with a stick.
It began to add more wood.

"Jerry..."

The Drac looked up.

"Use a piece of metal from my ship. Look in that pile
there."

The Drac nodded, crossed to the bundle of salvage
and pulled out a long, curving rod of shining steel. Davidge licked his lips nervously. "That'll do," he croaked.

The Drac shook its head. "Not." It continued sorting
through the wreckage. Davidge didn't see what it picked
up. It came back then. "Is trust?"

"Is trust."

"Good." And then, abruptly, the Drac was tying him
to the tree, securing his hands so they were tightly bound.

"Hey!"

The Drac did not pause; its hands were strong and
quick. "Is good you trust. Is also good I *not* trust. Is
much pain." The Drac looked into Davidge's eyes. "Is
must be done. I am sorry, Willy." Its face was troubled.

"I understand, Jerry. You're a goddamned lizard, but
you're not a stupid goddamned lizard. Let me have something to bite on. A stick, or a rag?"

The Drac nodded and found a clean stick. Davidge held it in his teeth.

The Drac went to the fire then and stirred it with the metal rod, shoving the rod into the hottest part of the flames. It came back to Davidge then and ripped his pants leg open wide and studied the wound dispassionately. *"Irkmann* is pink all over," the Drac remarked. One clawed finger traced the line of the wound on Davidge's calf. "Iss could be worse."

The Drac pulled a water bag down from the branch where it was hanging.

"Hey! That's our drinking water!"

"Is more where this came from. *Shizumaat* say . . . no, never mind what *Shizumaat* say." It began to pour water over the wound, washing away the sand and the dirt. "Iss good."

The Drac returned to the fire then and, using another piece of rag as a holder, picked up the hot metal rod. Davidge anchored his teeth on the stick, prepared to bite—

The Drac squatted down by his leg and pressed the metal bar against the wound.

At first it felt cold; then the sensation sorted itself out and it was burning. The fire was excruciating! Davidge screamed and bit the stick—it crunched apart—and passed out.

He came back up and out the other side, still screaming in agony, his leg was still on fire.

There was something cold and wet on his forehead, and a soft voice was saying, "Iss finished, Willy. Iss done."

"It still hurts, Jerry."

"Yes, I know, Willy." Davidge felt the Drac's hands on his leg. "Where hurt? Here?"

"No, lower."

"Here?"

"Aaagh! Yes!"

"Willy, look and see. What color is hurt?"

"Huh?"

"What color is hurt?" the Drac repeated.

"I don't . . ."

The Drac was insistent. *"Look and see.* What color is hurt?"

"It's . . ." Davidge *looked* at the pain in his leg. "It's red, no white—"

"Good. How big is hurt?"

"Huh? What are you doing?"

"Just answer questions. How big is hurt?"

Davidge *looked* again. "It's . . . it's as big as a . . . as a tree."

"Good. How heavy is hurt?"

"It's very heavy."

"How heavy?"

"A hundred kilos."

"What color is it now?"

Davidge *looked.* "It's yellow."

"How big?"

"Um, still as big as a tree. No, it's as big as a man— Jerry, what are you doing? It's getting smaller."

"Just answer the questions, *Irkmann.* How heavy is hurt?"

"Fifty klicks." Davidge wanted to laugh.

"Good, Willy, good. Look at pain again. What color is it?"

"It's, uh, it's blue." Davidge *looked* at the pain, let himself get inside of it. "No, it's green, or white . . ." It didn't really matter what color it was. The more he looked at it, the less it hurt.

"How big is it?"

"It's only the size of my leg now."

"You do good, Willy. How heavy is it?"

"One kilo. No! It doesn't weigh anything at all. It's gone! I mean . . ." Davidge opened his eyes and looked at Jerry. His eyes were shining. He laughed in startled delight. "I mean, I can still feel it, but it doesn't hurt. What did you do?"

"Iss did nothing," said the Drac. "Iss Willy did all."

"No, you did something, didn't you? Tell me what you did."

"Is only ask questions. You did all. Healing can start now without pain to get in way. Healing starts when pain complete. I ask you questions. You look. You complete pain. Pain is completed when you look at it."

"I don't believe it . . ." Davidge trailed off.

"Whether you believe or not is not matter. It works without you believe."

"Is that . . . Did that come from the *Talman*, Jerry? Is that from *Shizumaat?*"

The Drac stood up without answering. "I go get dinner now," it said and left the clearing. Davidge stared after him, confused. "Now, what the hell? Last week, I couldn't get him to shut up about *Shizumaat.*"

18

THE MOCK TURTLE meat hissed and crackled over the fire. It spat hot grease into the embers and gave off the most incredibly delicious smells.

"Oh, God, that smells good. I'm in heaven," moaned Davidge.

"Heaven?" asked the Drac. "What is heaven?"

"It's where you go after you, uh . . ." Davidge stopped himself. He'd made it a rule not to talk about anything religious with the Drac. Instead, he said, "It's the good place. The best place to be."

"Oh," said the Drac. It cut off two large slices of meat, one for Davidge and one for itself, and laid them on pieces of the Mock Turtle shell. The Drac called the creature a *cuca*. Davidge hadn't asked why.

"Thank you, Jerry," Davidge said as the Drac passed him his meat. He held the plate up to his nose and inhaled deeply. "I never thought I'd smell anything this good again." He cut off a bite with his knife and chewed it slowly, savoring every bit of its chewy red taste. It was a lot like beef or lamb, except it had a sharp, almost fatty overtaste. Buttery? Almost. Davidge took another bite. It wasn't as tough as he'd expected. It was chewy and it had a rich flavor and—

He held out his plate to the Drac, "Jerry, would you cut me another slice please?"

The Drac was still working on its first helping, but it

put its meal aside and hacked off another chunk of meat for the human. "You eat like pig, *Irkmann.*"

"Huh?" Davidge took the plate of *cuca*-shell from the Drac. "Well, your eating habits aren't the greatest either."

The Drac ignored the retort. "Iss good for pig. Iss not good for Drac." Jerry looked up. "Iss good for human to eat like pig?"

"Hey! This is the first real meal I've had since crashing on this stinkball." And then Davidge realized what the lizard was asking. He added, "This is *real* food, Drac. I'm descended from a long line of omnivores. Although I think my branch of the family was mostly carnivorous. We like meat a lot."

"Do all humans like meat?"

David nodded. He wasn't about to try and explain vegetarianism. "It's in our ancestry. Humans used to hunt for meat."

"Used to? Humans do not eat meat anymore?"

"No, humans still eat meat."

"But you don't hunt?" The Drac looked puzzled.

"No. Now we just keep herds."

"Keep. Herds?" The Drac blinked. "Explain, please."

"We raise animals. We breed them."

"Oh." The Drac looked relieved. "Iss misunderstand. Then you release them for hunt?"

"No. We don't hunt. We raise them until they're big enough to eat, then we . . . eat them."

The Drac looked startled, shocked—horrified. A whole panoply of expressions flickered across its face. Davidge was learning to read Drac expressions, but even these were too fast and furious for him to identify. Clearly, though, the Drac was upset.

"Not *gavey, Irkmann.* Humans raise captives to eat?"

"Well . . . yes, sort of. But Jerry—they're only animals."

"Is not *only* animals! Is *life!* Is brother in creation!" The Drac was disgusted. "You eat brothers!!"

Davidge was annoyed. "You eat animals!" he accused. "You're eating meat that I killed!"

"Not same thing, *Irkmann!*"

"Well, I wish you'd explain it to me. I don't see the difference, Drac!"

"Hunt respects..." The Drac hesitated, looking for the word, "—respects inside-idea-of-person."

"Inside-idea-of-person? Do you mean spirit?"

"Is that *Irk* word? Hunt respects spirit."

"Yeah, I see what you're saying."

"Not hunt, eat captives instead—is like *eating slaves!*" The Drac's expression was twisted in disgust.

Davidge didn't answer. There wasn't anything he could say. The Drac had clearly won the moral point here. There was no way to explain that animals didn't have souls or didn't feel the pain or—

I don't know. Do animals have souls? For that matter, do the Dracs?

"Hey!" said Davidge, looking up abruptly.

"What is it now, *Irkmann*?"

"You said something about life being brothers."

"I not say it. *Shizumaat* say it," the Drac admitted sullenly.

"Well... does that apply to *Irkmann* too? Is that why you saved my life?"

"You not my brother, *Irkmann!* Maybe human and Drac be brothers of life. Maybe someday other *Irkmann* learn it and war be over. But you and I, not! Slave-eater!"

Davidge looked at his half-finished plate of meat. He fingered the hard cuca-shell thoughtfully. *I'll wager a nickel I can tell you something about Drac history, Jerry,* he said to himself. *I wonder how many died in the Drac holocaust.*

"Then, why did you save my life?" he asked.

Jerry Shigan did not answer. The Drac just shrugged and turned away.

"I guess you just like having me around, huh? You like my face, right?"

"I *not* like your face. I not like your whole ugly head."

"Then why did you save me, Jerry?" Davidge insisted.

"Because I not like that thing's ugly head even more than I not like yours."

Davidge suppressed his answer. Calling the lizard a spoiled hatchling would only prolong its sulk. "Okay, you win, Jerry," he said in resignation and tossed his plate onto a nearby rock; it clattered with a loud sound. Abruptly, Davidge turned and looked at it, then picked it up again and rapped the piece of shell with his fingers. "Hey!"

Jerry didn't look up.

"No—Jerry, look!"

The Drac turned its head and looked. Its expression was masked.

Davidge held up the shell. "This is it! This is the answer!"

"What was the question?" hissed the Drac.

"That sand pit was surrounded with these shells! Even that *thing* under the ground couldn't bite through this. I'll bet these shells are even meteor proof!" Davidge grinned. "Jerry, I'll say it again. Where would you be without me?"

The Drac continued chewing for a moment, then looked at Davidge expressionlessly. It was totally unimpressed with his genius.

"Back home," it said.

19

THIS TIME THE SHELTER was built around a framework of tree limbs, shingled with cuca-shells. A bony protuberance inside each shell made it possible to hook them one upon another. The purple vines from the trees could be used to tie them in place. The shelter might creak in a strong wind, but it would keep out the rain. And very likely the meteorites as well.

They'd find out soon enough.

Davidge put a deep bed of stones in the center of the hut for the fire and an opening at the top of the dome for the smoke to escape. Then he dug drainage trenches around the outside to keep water from running into the shelter. Now, if he could only figure out some way to build a bed that was off the ground. But first, he wanted to build a smokehouse for the cuca meat. There just wasn't enough time in a day to do everything that needed doing.

He paused to rest in his labors and looked over at the Drac.

Jerry was reading the *Talman* again.

Davidge resented that, not that Jerry spent so much time reading—but that he wouldn't *share* it. It was very odd, and also very frustrating because the lizard seemed so willing to share everything else.

"Hey, Professor! How 'bout a little help?"

The Drac looked over at him, then reluctantly hung the *Talman* around its neck again.

"Don't you ever get tired of that book?"

"No," said Jerry. It walked over to him slowly. "What do you want?"

"What's in it, anyway?" asked Davidge. "You never talk about it anymore."

"It iss not for you." The Drac stooped to pick up a shell.

"Oh, fer Crissakes, Jerry! Give me a break."

"It iss not for you," the Drac repeated. "Where do you want to put these?"

Davidge resisted the obvious answer. Anger didn't work on the Drac. He was learning that. All it did was force the lizard into sullenness. He took a breath and said quietly, "No. Tell me about the *Talman*."

Jerry shook its head.

"No, I mean it. I want to learn. I'm learning your language, Jerry. Teach me how to read your book."

The Drac simply stared at him. "I mean it too, Willy. It iss not for you."

"I don't *gavey* that. What is it? *Shizumaat* is too good for us humans. That it?"

"No, not too good for humans. Too good for *you*." Jerry turned away, carrying the cuca-shell over to the half-finished smokehouse.

"Huh?" Davidge followed him. "Since when did you become a judge of character? Who died and appointed you God?"

Jerry laid the shell down carefully on the ground. It turned back to Davidge and said, "You have forgotten what you said about *Shizumaat*?"

"I never said anything about *Shizumaat*!"

"Then who eats the *kiz* of scavenger pigs?"

"Huh—?" And then Davidge remembered. "Oh, God,

is that what this is all about? You son of a . . . ! You've been holding that against me? You high-handed hypocritical half-wit!" The Drac remained impassive. And then Davidge remembered something else. "Do you think it was right for you to say what you said about Mickey Mouse?"

The Drac blinked. And blinked again. It said, "That was wrong too. I should not have said it."

"No, you shouldn't have." Davidge's eyes met Jerry's. He felt his own shame then. "And I'm sorry too. I didn't mean what I said about *Shizumaat*. I was angry, I wanted to hurt you. I was wrong, Jerry. Please forgive me."

The Drac shook its head. "No. You must forgive me. I should have acted better. I have studied *Talman*. I should have known better than to return anger with anger. You *must* forgive me. The greater error was mine."

Davidge stopped and studied the Drac. He'd never seen the lizard act like this before. Jerry had saved his life and never said anything about it; but this—Davidge felt himself at a loss. He didn't know what to say to this. So he *looked* inside himself instead—and said what he felt; he reached out and put his hands on the lizard-man's shoulders, "Jerry, you are my friend."

The Drac frowned in puzzlement. It didn't know the word *friend*. Davidge had never taught it. *What was the phrase the Drac had used?*

"You are my brother-in-life," Davidge continued. "There should be nothing between us that needs forgiveness. But whatever forgiveness must be given, I give it to you freely."

Jerry's eyes were bright. "I thank you, Davidge, for the great gift. You have never called me 'friend' before. I did not know. I thought you were inside-angry with me, because you have never mentioned your Mickey

Mooze again. I would share *Shizumaat* with you, if you would share Mickey Mooze with me."

"I would be honored."

Jerry hesitated for a moment, then lifted the *Talman* on its chain from around its neck and placed it carefully around Davidge's neck.

"Jerry, what—?"

"The *Talman* must be given to the pupil. I thus become the Master. I am unworthy, but there is nobody else here."

Davidge raised his hand and cradled the tiny golden book in his fingers. He did not *gavey* all the honor that he had just been given, but he definitely felt the joy!

"Thank you, Jerry. Thank you for trusting me again."

═══════20

THERE WERE EIGHTY-ONE SYMBOLS in the Drac alphabet.

This much Davidge could understand.

After that, it got harder.

The Drac kept trying to tell him something about what each character meant, but none of it made sense to Davidge. Why should the *aa* sound also mean *strongly interested?* And why was it important to know? Couldn't he just learn the words first?

The Drac shook his head in annoyance. "No, no, no! Willy—get it into your ugly head! *Gavey* means 'understand' because *aa* means what it means. You would not *gava* when you want to *gavey,* would you?"

"No, of course not," Davidge agreed, wondering what *gava* meant. "But I still don't understand—I don't *gavey* why I have to know that *aa* means 'strongly interested' and *ee* means 'fearful' and all the other meanings. Why should the vowels and consonants have meanings of their own? Please, Jerry, just teach me the words first, and how to read them in the *Talman.*"

At that, the Drac threw up its hands in disgust and started muttering a stream of invective to itself like a distraught Cuban bandleader. It stamped off into the woods, shaking its head.

"Jerry, wait—!"

"Is not your fault, *Irkmann,*" Jerry called back. "*Shi-*

zumaat say, 'There are no poor students, there are only poor teachers!'"

Davidge didn't understand it.

But he wasn't willing to give up. The Drac had tried very hard to get him to see that each character had its own 'inside-idea.' Inner quality? Spirit? Davidge wasn't sure. Even with Jerry's clumsy attempts at pantomime, there were some notions that simply wouldn't come clear.

Why should each character represent not just a sound, but a spiritual quality as well? What did that have to do with the words?

The best that he could figure out was that the vowels represented the emotional qualities of a concept, as well as its level of energy. The consonants determined the physical qualities of the concept.

Hmm...

That suggested something interesting. Davidge sat up straight with the realization. If that was true, then just as human scholars could create new words out of Greek and Latin roots, so could Drac scholars create new words by determining the emotional and physical qualities of the thing the word was to represent.

Okay, that made sense. Sort of. But it still didn't answer the other question. Why couldn't you just learn the words first? That was where they were stuck. He couldn't even ask the question anymore without risking Jerry's wrath.

All that Davidge could do was practice his pronunciation tables, his vowels and consonants. Over and over again. At least, they had a natural rhythm. He could practice his pronunciation by singing. He called it his "Cracklin' Dracon Blues."

But he couldn't understand how such a language could come into being. Who made up the first words? Who chose the meanings for the vowels and consonants in the first place? Where did it all come from?

It was while reciting the Drac vowels to himself that he realized what he'd been missing all along. He dropped what he was doing and went in search of Jerry. "Hey, Drac!"

The Drac looked up from its work; it was boiling fat into oil for their lamps. "What is it, *Irkmann?*"

"The Drac language. It's supposed to be *sung*, isn't it?"

"Sung? Not *gavey*. What is 'sung'?"

"Um—you *sing* a *song*. Like this: '*When I was a lad in Venusport, I took up the local indoor sport....*'" Davidge's bass rang across the clearing.

The Drac stared at him in astonishment.

"Right?" asked Davidge. "You don't talk it, you *sing* it?"

"Willy, you are telling me that *Irkmann* has different words for 'talk' and . . . 'sing'?"

"In Drac, it's the same thing, isn't it?"

"In Engleesh, it is not?"

The two of them stared at each other for an instant— and then both burst out laughing at the same time. Hearty guffaws came chortling up out of Davidge's chest; the Drac hissed and smirked and pounded its knee.

"Sometime, Willy, I will tell you about Vamma's Assumption. A very old story. Very funny. Vamma was almost as big a fool as you and I. We make assumptions from inside our own—" The Drac thumped its forehead. "—from inside our own heads."

"You do that, Jerry, and I'll tell you about the leprechauns and the penguin. That's also a very old story. But—" Davidge waved his hands excitedly. "I think I *gavey* now. You sing the words because it's not the word that's important. It's the inner meaning, right? And if you don't know the meanings of the letters, you can't hear the inner meaning, right?"

"Irkmann, you are not as stupid as you are ugly."

"Yes, I am! I should have realized this a lot sooner. I see it now. It's not enough to just say *Shizumaat.* You have to sing it, like so: *Shiz-u-maat!"* He grinned at the Drac. "Right?"

"Irkmann," said the Drac. "That is the first time you say the name that it does not sound like a curse falling from your mouth."

"Thank you, Jerry."

"Thank *you,* Willy!" The Drac was beaming. "Now, you may teach me something from Mickey Mooze, please?"

"Now?"

"Now, please. Is trade, share for share, right? I teach you from *Shizumaat* and you teach me from Mickey Mooze."

Oh, shit. Davidge gulped and nodded, suddenly at a loss. How could he explain this one? If he told the truth about Mickey Mouse, it might be an insult to Drac from which the relationship might never recover—the implication being that an animated rodent was considered the equal of *Shizumaat.*

"Okay, Jerry, but you have to sit down for this. Mickey Mouse was born a long time ago. He was . . . Well, let me put it this way. He never taught anybody anything in his life—except by example."

"Very wise," nodded Jerry.

"Right," said Davidge, wishing he were anyplace else right now. "Anyway, uh—people used to come to Mickey Mouse because they were sick; not in the body, but in the . . . spirit—and not sick, really, as much as *tired.*

People would come to Mickey Mouse because they were tired and didn't even know they were tired. *Gavey,* so far?"

"Ae!"

"Good. So Mickey Mouse would . . . uh, dance, or perform a—a dance or performance." Davidge felt like a fool, but he kept on. "—and the people would watch. And sometimes they would even laugh."

"Laugh?" asked the Drac. "They would laugh at Mickey Mooze?"

"Uh, yes. They were supposed to—because the dances were supposed to be funny." .

"Good!" said Jerry. *"Shizumaat* say, 'Laughter is best for healing.' *Shizumaat* tell funny story too."

"Uh, really?" Davidge began to breathe a little easier. "Anyway, Mickey Mooze—I mean, Mouse; now you've got me doing it—anyway, Mickey Mouse would make people laugh and forget that they were tired. Afterward, they would go home and realize that Mickey Mouse represented . . . um, happiness and joy and love and enthusiasm and—and taking a stand and not giving up." Davidge bit one knuckle speculatively. So far, he still hadn't told a lie, but he wouldn't want it tested in a court of law either.

"Go on, *Irkmann!"* Jerry insisted.

"Well, anyway, there were these people who worked for Mickey Mouse, a lot of them. And their job was to . . . um, sort of repeat Mickey's dances and performances for other people—and they did it by—um, making films of Mickey Mouse, so everybody everywhere could see him. At first nobody realized what Mickey Mouse was really doing; they just thought he was a clown, a performer. But people liked to see his films and it was only later that people realized that they liked to see his dances not just because they were happy and funny, but because they reminded them of love and enthusiasm and not giving up. And that's how Mickey Mouse taught people about life and what it could be like—but he never said it *should* be. The choice was always up to the viewer. The student." Davidge wiped his forehead. Boy, was he stretching that one—

The Drac nodded. "Is very powerful teacher, your Mickey Mooze. Very smart. Please to give to me a *ko-ahn* of Mickey Mooze to think about."

"A *ko-ahn?*"

"A thinking-sentence—very puzzling—about which the thinking about produces . . . light-in-the-thinking."

"You must mean a puzzle. Like a paradox? A paradox that produces enlightenment?"

"*Ae!* En-light-en-ment. The lifting of burden of heavy confusion. Please to give me a thinking-sentence from Mickey Mooze."

"Urk—" said Davidge. His mind went suddenly blank. All he could remember was, "Uh— 'Today is Wednesday. You know what that means? Anything Can Happen Day!'"

"Anything Can Happen Day?" The Drac looked happily puzzled.

"Uh, right."

"*Ae!* Good! This is very puzzling. This is good. I will think about it. 'Today is Wednesday. You know what that means? Anything Can Happen Day!'"

Davidge had to get up suddenly and leave. He was having a choking fit.

21

THEIR DAYS FELL INTO A RITUAL. In the mornings they would do the work of the day, hunting or repairing or building. Then they would break for lunch, the big meal of the day. After that, they would go out onto the bluff overlooking the badlands and Jerry would teach Willy from the *Talman*. Or Willy would teach Jerry something from Earth legends.

Jerry taught Willy about Vamma's Assumption.

Willy taught Jerry about Wil. E. Coyote who went to extraordinary lengths to destroy himself.

Jerry taught Willy about the Gift of the Enemy.

Willy taught Jerry about The Revenge of the Bunny, and how revenge is a dish best served funny.

Jerry taught Willy about The Forgiveness of the Child.

And Willy taught Jerry about The Wrath of the Duck.

What amazed Davidge was not that he was learning to speak and think like a Drac—that was what he set out to do—but that he was discovering all sorts of other truths in the most *unlikely* places.

He mentioned it to Jerry one afternoon, in an oblique way. "I'm starting to see things differently, Jerry. I'm seeing things *inside*. *Gavey?*"

"Say more, please?"

"If a rock falls—I used to see just a rock falling. Now I see gravity. If you yell at me—I used to see just your anger. Now, I see your caring. You cannot be angry with someone unless you care."

"*Ae!* Very good. Is amazing, no? That *Irkmann* is capable of inner-seeing?" Jerry hissed its delight. "I knew that *Shizumaat's* teachings were powerful, but never *this* powerful. This is a story I will never be able to tell."

"Why not?"

"Who would believe it?"

"So? Who would believe that I told a goddamned lizard about Mickey Mouse?"

"*Ae!*" Jerry nodded. "I must admit something here too, Willy. I think you are a better student than I am. I think you learn *Shizumaat* better than I learn Mickey Mooze. I have still not puzzled out 'Anything Can Happen Day!'"

"Um, well, I'm sorry about that Jerry."

"No, no, do not explain. I will en-light-en-ment this one myself."

"Good. I'm not sure I can explain it to you anyway. It's like jazz. If you have to have it explained, you don't understand it."

"Jazz?"

"Never mind." Davidge opened the *Talman* again and began to sing. The words floated out over the harsh rocks. The huge red sun of Fyrine bathed the harsh landscape in waves of crimson light.

"*Yesli raz dzram va delo, pust raz va dzram ohi del. Da pust va protanyat bulv ot va, lubo ix dzodini.*"

Jerry nodded. "Now, translate please."

"Urk," said Davidge. "I *gavey,* but I'm not sure I can explain. In English, I can only approximate."

The Drac waited patiently.

"All right, here goes. 'If one receives evil at the hands of another, let one not do evil in return. Rather, let him extend to the enemy'—the closest English word is 'love', but that's not quite right, because what *this* means is the comradeship of being a brother-in-life, and 'love' only sometimes means that."

"Yes, yes. Go on," Jerry prompted.

"Uh, right. 'Rather, let him extend 'love' to the enemy, so that love might unite them.'" Davidge looked at Jerry. "That's in the human *Talman* too."

"Of course. Truth is truth. Even ugly *Irkmann* is not too stupid to recognize truth when it comes up and bites him on the ass like a sand-demon."

"I should never have taught you how to swear in English," Davidge muttered.

"It makes for useful teaching tool when you teach a '*shyskopf.*'" Jerry smirked. "Like you are now."

"Huh?"

"Your singing of the *Talman* was . . . not good."

"Not good? I've never been better!"

"That is unfortunate truth, *Irkmann*. You have never been better, but it is still not good enough. You offend the ears and the spirit."

"I offend?!" Davidge was honestly hurt.

"The truth is always painful. A performance like that in the High Halls would get you . . . What is Earth equivalent? Staked out on an anthill for blasphemy." The Drac reached over and touched Davidge's arm. "Listen—"

Jerry closed its eyes and began to sing the exact same verse. Davidge could hear the difference instantly. There was a note of *mournfulness* in the sound, a strange sweet sadness. It was as if someone beyond Jerry were speaking through the song and saying, "I am sorry to tell you that there is such a thing as deliberate pain in this universe, but you must know that there is *evil* and that it is a seductive emotion. It will tempt you and if you give in, you will belong to it. Return love for evil—it is the harder path, but you will never be enslaved to the animal feelings within."

The words echoed off into silence and sorrow, leaving the question hanging in the air.

The next verse contained the answer. Jerry hadn't even begun to sing it and suddenly, Davidge understood how it had to be sung. It was a joyous verse. It said that evil is the silliest action of all because it produces the most useless result in the universe. The only good thing that you can do with evil is laugh at it. Like Mickey Mouse! Somehow—paradoxically—it all fit together in a mad, wonderful pattern. The truth is the truth and even an ugly Earthman will recognize it when it sneaks up and bites him on the ass!

Davidge opened his mouth to sing along with Jerry when something caught his eye, a sparkling of lights in the sky.

"Oh, shit! Jerry!"

The Drac opened its eyes, startled, angered at the rudeness of the interruption—

"Zeerki!" shouted Davidge. *"Zeerki!"*

22

THE TWO OF THEM ran as fast as they could, up the slope and toward the trees; except there was something wrong with the way Jerry was running. Davidge had to help the Drac over some of the rocks.

The first of the meteorites struck the ground ahead of them even before they reached the cover of the trees. By the time they were among the massive trunks, the ground all around them was exploding. It sounded like an artillery barrage. The ancient trees popped and splintered, spewing jagged pieces of wood in all directions. Branches broke off from the canopy above and came crashing roughly to the ground. Clouds of dust and debris rose up from the ground. The air was full of flying things, leaves and bits of moss and stinging black particles.

Davidge and the Drac ran, scrambled, ducked—narrowly missed an explosion big enough to demolish a house—and kept moving—

Oh, God! Would the shelter hold?

"Come on, Jerry! Move your scaly ass! What's the matter with you, anyway?"

"Unh—my ass is not—" The Drac slowed down to climb over a fallen trunk that Davidge had seen it leap over only a couple weeks ago. "—scaly."

A meteor hit behind them then and pieces of wood

caromed off the trees over their heads. They both flattened themselves onto the ground. Davidge was up first and running without looking back.

The shelter was just ahead. The ground around it looked like popcorn was exploding out of it. Davidge dashed and leaped and skidded into the dome. Meteorites were richocheting off the rocks and smacking into the ground and the trees like gunshots. The dome was twanging like the inside of a kettle drum.

"Come on, Jerry!"

Davidge turned around and looked. The Drac was nowhere to be seen. His stomach lurched. "Oh, God, no." Davidge was already scrambling back out of the dome, shouting, "Jerry! Dammit! Where the hell are you?"

There! The Drac was still on its feet, coming through the horror. But too slowly. It moved heavily.

Davidge ran to it and grabbed it by the arm. He pulled the Drac along roughly. "Jesus Christ, you lizard son of a bitch! What the hell is wrong?"

He practically dragged Jerry the last few feet into the shelter. The two of them collapsed on the floor, gasping and croaking for breath, while the world cracked like it was coming apart at the seams. It sounded like the inside of the Fourth of July. The meteorites smacked and pounded on the cuca shells all around them.

Davidge rolled over on his side and stared at Jerry. "What do I have to do, carry you?"

"I am sorry, Willy."

Davidge was too annoyed to forgive. All he could think to say was, "Here we are, living like animals, and you get so fat you can hardly move. You'll never conquer the universe in that state, Jerry."

Jerry's eyes narrowed. "Conquer the universe? My

people were here a thousand years before yours."

The barrage outside suddenly doubled in intensity. The Drac covered its ears.

So did Davidge. He had to shout to be heard above the din. "In case you didn't hear about it, we legally annexed this star system!"

"You *invaded* this star system!"

"Bullshit! You're the aggressors!"

"No! We are explorers! We are founders of worlds!"

Something boomed outside, rocking the shelter badly. Several shells broke off, leaving gaping holes in one of the walls.

Davidge ignored it, he was too angry, he screamed, "And what do you think we are, Toadface? Homebodies! We've settled twice as many worlds as you!"

"Exactly!" shouted Jerry. "You spread like disease!"

"Yeah? Well I'd like to know what you're going to do about it!"

"You see what we do, *Irkmann*. We fight!"

"Yah? Is that how you follow the teaching of *Shizumaat?* Is that how you return love for evil?"

"At least you recognize your own *wrongness!* Slaveeater! We fight when there is no alternative."

"Look what's talking! Look at you, Jerry! You're no fighter. You wouldn't last a week without me."

"Hah! It is I who saved your life, *Irkmann!* You forget. You owe your stupid ugly existence to me, remember?"

More of the cuca shells flew off then. The ground was shaking like an earthquake. The shelter was threatening to collapse around them.

"Yeah, okay Draco! Let's see how well you can survive on your own. Get your ugly face out of my shelter!"

"Your shelter?"

"Yeah! I built it! Now get out!"

Davidge leapt across the intervening space and grabbed at Jerry, trying to drag the goddamn lizard—and this time he meant it—toward the entrance of the shelter. Outside, the meteors continued to whistle and whine and smack into the ground like rockets.

Jerry struck Davidge a sweeping blow of its open hand, knocking him backward into the opposite wall of the dome. Davidge fell against one of the rocks they had used as a foundation, opening a deep cut. He paused only long enough to touch his fingers to his head, then leapt to his feet and charged at Jerry.

They fell together, grappling, rolling over, punching and kicking at each other. Davidge was enraged, he wanted to *kill*.

Suddenly, there was silence.

The meteor shower was over.

Davidge and Jerry stopped and looked at each other; they ceased their struggle, lying in an exhausted embrace, face to face—like the last time they had escaped from the meteors. Davidge didn't want to be reminded.

He felt stupid and ashamed. He'd said things he hadn't meant; he'd said them to deliberately hurt the Drac. He straightened up, disentangling himself from Jerry's passive embrace and moved over to lean against the opposite wall.

He put his face in his hands and *mourned*. How was he ever going to apologize for *this?* He wrapped one hand around the *Talman* hanging around his neck and wished he had learned it better. There must be something in the tiny golden book—

Jerry was raising itself into a sitting position, slowly.

"Are you all right?" Davidge asked.

"I will not die," Jerry said slowly. "At least, not to-day." Its tone of voice was flat, and Davidge couldn't tell what the Drac was thinking. "I think I understand now, Willy."

"Huh—? Understand what?"

"Today is Wednesday, isn't it? Anything Can Happen Day. *Ae gavey!*"

And then, relieved, Davidge started laughing—and crying at the same time.

23

DAVIDGE WANTED TO APOLOGIZE, to beg for forgiveness. But the Drac wouldn't let him finish his speech.

"No, Willy. Now iss my turn. You teach me thiss." Jerry put both its hands on Davidge's shoulders and spoke with the solemnity of a ritual, "You are my friend. There should be nothing between us that needs forgiveness. But whatever forgiveness must be given, I give it to you freely."

"Thank you, Jerry. You damn fool Drac."

"There iss nothing to thank, ugly *Irkmann*." It added, "I am merely return the gift. I return love for..." The Drac stopped to consider its next words. "You are not evil, Willy. Actions are evil, sometimes, but you are not, so I can only return love for love with you."

"*Ae. Gavey.*"

After a long joyous moment, the two of them broke apart. Davidge looked around the mess of the dome and said, "I didn't do such a good job of building, after all."

"It was good enough to save our lives."

Davidge nodded. "Yah. I guess so." He looked over at Jerry. "Is there a word for rage? Anger-madness?"

"*Ae.* Many words. Too many." The Drac admitted sadly, "Dracs know about evil actions too much."

"Like slave-eaters?"

Jerry looked ashamed. "I should not have called you that. It is a very bad thing to call someone."

"Your people had a war once, didn't they? Where they ate the losers, right?"

Jerry nodded, ashamed.

"My people too," Davidge admitted. "Too many times."

"Slave-eaters?"

"Not quite, but just as bad. Whole populations were put to death, just because they said different prayers."

"Different—prayers?"

"*Aah*. Different . . . interpretations of truth."

"Not understand, Willy. Truth not need . . . interpretation."

"Right. Try it this way. It is as if Drac were to war on Drac because they argued over what *Shizumaat* said."

"Argue over *Shizumaat*—?" Jerry considered it. "I think I would rather be a slave-eater."

"Yeah, me too." Davidge smiled wryly, "At least, you'd eat regular."

The Drac looked disgusted.

"Sorry, Jerry—I really am. I think I'm starting to go crazy here. Maybe we both are. I don't know. I don't know what a *sane* Drac acts like."

Jerry didn't answer.

"What do you think?"

"I am not sane Drac, Willy. What I think is not matter."

"Not sane? Of course, you are!"

The Drac merely shook its head. "Not now." It added, "You only think that you are not. I *know* that I am not."

"Okay, have it your way, but what you think still matters."

"No, it doesn't. Not now."

"Not now? I don't understand."

The Drac didn't answer.

"Jerry—? I thought we traded forgiveness."

"We did. Thiss has nothing to do with forgiveness, *Irkmann*. Iss just so. What I think is not matter."

"Yes, it does."

The Drac shook its head again.

"Well, I think we have to start moving. I think we've stayed here too long. The cuca are getting harder to find anyway. And besides..."

"Aaeh?"

"—I don't think we're alone out here, do you?"

"Of course, we are alone."

Davidge shook his head. "No, Jerry—I keep thinking I'm hearing ships. Maybe you can't hear notes that high. I can. It's like a hissing in my ears. You can hear it on Earth when a shuttle comes in if you're in a quiet enough place. I hear it in my sleep, Jerry, but when I wake up, I still hear it, so I know I'm not dreaming."

"You dream awake then."

"No, I know what I heard. It was the hissing of a ship in the atmosphere. But even if you're right, even if I am dreaming awake, we still can't stay here, Jerry. We're going crazy. If this planet doesn't kill us, we'll kill each other."

The Drac didn't answer.

"We've got to go look for help," Davidge insisted. He knew he was right about this, the passion was rising in his voice. "Listen to me, Jerry. We're falling into a rut. Do you know what a rut is? That's a grave with the ends knocked out. We've got to put some kind of purpose back in our lives."

Jerry shook its head. "I have purpose."

"What? Just sitting around getting fat?"

"If that is what you think, then that is what you think." Jerry stood up and walked to the door of the hut. "There are still some things *Irkmann* does not know."

24

DAVIDGE ARGUED FOR A WEEK. It was to no avail. Jerry was adamant. Davidge could go if he wished. Jerry was going to stay with the shelter. Nothing Davidge could say would change the Drac's mind; neither would the Drac explain its refusal to travel.

It just repeated quietly, whenever Davidge pressed the issue, "What iss, iss. What iss not, iss not. Rocks are hard, water is wet, and I am not moving."

Davidge sighed with disgust and gave up. Instead, he concentrated on repairing and reinforcing the shelter. Jerry sat within, sewing him a cuca-skin coat and bundle. The preparations for Davidge's journey took longer than he expected, more than two weeks.

On the morning of his departure, Davidge looked at the Drac speculatively and asked, "Jerry, are you all right? Is there something you're not telling me?"

"I am—fine," said the Drac. "It iss just . . . season."

Why don't I believe you? Davidge wondered. "Are you sure you won't change your mind and come with me?"

Jerry shook its head.

"Any chance is better than no chance.".

The Drac looked at Davidge with sad eyes.

"There's something wrong, isn't there?"

"Iss nothing wrong. I tell you again. Just go, ugly *Irkmann!* Just go!"

"If I find help, I'll come back for you."

"And if you do not?"

"Then, I guess . . . each of us will die alone."

The Drac nodded.

"Well . . ." Davidge waved half-heartedly. "So long, Jerry."

The Drac didn't answer. It was staring moodily off into the distance.

Davidge paused a moment more, as if wanting to say something else, as if wanting to give the Drac one more chance to respond, then, when no further response was forthcoming, he turned and strode angrily away into the forest. He felt somehow incomplete.

Dammit!

But there was nothing else he could do, so he kept on walking.

All right, to hell with the goddamn lizard then. So what! Who needed a friend anyway? Davidge shouldered his bundle and pushed forward through the Dead Forest, up a rocky slope and into the cold wind. It stung his eyes and scrubbed at his skin. He drew the collar of his cuca-skin coat tight around his neck, and turned around once to look backward.

Far away, under the trees, was the shelter he had thought of as home for so long. It looked very small and vulnerable. There was no sign of Jerry, not even smoke from the fire. Davidge hesitated. Something told him—

"No! I'm sure that there are people somewhere on this planet, either Drac or human! They're not looking for us—we've got to look for them. And if the goddamn lizard won't get off his fat scaly butt, then it's up to me to save both our lives."

He turned and walked on.

Out of sheer boredom, he opened the *Talman* and picked a page at random. He began to memorize the verse on the page, practicing not only his pronunciation, but his singing as well. He'd show Jerry.

The slope gave way to a black, volcanic desert—a frozen sea of hard brittle rock. Davidge stopped and stared. For how many eons had this process been continuing? It looked like something out of one of Dante's nightmares.

Here, the lava had boiled and flowed and solidified, boiled and flowed a second time, a third. The ground had shaken and cracked and broken the rocks into huge, sheer-sided slabs; some of the cracks were so glassy they were like mirrors, catching the glare of the day in bright, glimmering pools. In some places, there even seemed to be colors in them.

If the boiling of the rock were not enough, the landscape had also been attacked by meteors and pocked with craters of all sizes—craters within craters, overlapping like spattering raindrops, only instead of rain, it was the molten core of the planet that was being sprayed across the ground.

The meteors had come again and again. The lava must have flowed many times too, and been cracked by earthquakes many times. The planet was scarred like a warrior—

—but it moaned like a banshee.

The wind swept across the lava like an army of tormented souls seeking escape from Hell.

Davidge shuddered and pushed on. If he wanted a fire to sleep by, he'd have to get off this lava field before nightfall.

The lava fields gave way to barren plateau.

Davidge found some dry brush and made himself a sparse fire. He lay as close to it as he dared, wondering where he was and why he was alone. Why bother to exist, he wondered, if this is all that existence can be?

The wind howled in the distance. It sounded like wolves and widows and once it even sounded like a warp drive. He sat up to listen to that, but the sound was already gone.

The next day he continued, and the plateau opened out onto a dried-out delta. Traced across the landscape were hundreds of dry tributaries snaking through the parched earth like empty veins. Far across the delta, a gigantic crater rose ominously against the horizon and the darkening sky beyond.

He opened the *Talman* again and chose a new verse. He realized, with an odd satisfaction, that by now he probably knew more about the Drac culture than any other human being had ever learned. What a terrific joke! Captain Willis Davidge was now humanity's greatest living authority on the Drac culture.

The only problem was, humanity didn't know it, or even where to find him.

Damn, it was cold.

Davidge kept walking and singing, singing and walking. It took him the better part of a day to get to the base of the giant crater. The way was studded with steaming, smoking, bubbling pools of mud. He had to pick his path carefully.

Finally, just ahead of him, he spotted an opening. A gully had eroded its way through the crater wall, leaving a wide pass into the center of the crater itself.

Davidge debated with himself: He could try to cross the crater—it would be shorter than going around—but there was no guarantee of a pass on the opposite side. This might be the only real entrance.

It was worth a look, at least.

He climbed up into the crater. Ahead, he could see columns of steam rising up into the air, and he could hear a noise. A faint tapping. It was a metallic sound.

What the—? Davidge hastened his pace.

The center of the crater looked like a molten sea. It bubbled and heaved and smoked. And it smelled of rotten eggs and worse. He climbed down cautiously, listening for the elusive tapping sound. It was just ahead. The floor of the crater was warm, unpleasantly so, but he could manage.

There was something bright on the crater floor.

Davidge moved toward it, unbelievingly.

A small metallic cylinder.

Red and white.

With the words *Coca-Cola* stencilled on it in flowing script.

He picked it up in astonishment and stared.

He shook it. It was dry inside.

He put his nose to the can and sniffed. There was just the faintest hint of an almost-forgotten, familiar sweet scent.

"Dammit! Dammit! Dammit!" Davidge flung the can from him as hard as he could. The light aluminium container bounced and skittered across the rocks and disappeared into the smoky distance. "We missed them! Goddamn you, Jerry! We could have been saved! We missed them!"

He wandered forward. There were other bits of litter here: another aluminum can, a torn part of a magazine— Davidge clutched it eagerly, stuffing it inside his jacket— a greasy rag, an old shoe. They were barely visible in the steaming mist of the crater floor, but they were evidence that human beings had stood here once.

Davidge's face was haggard. He didn't know whether to cry or laugh, whether to be joyous at the evidence or raging at his failure to make contact.

Just ahead was a rigid metal pole protruding from the ground. It was about four feet high and had a metal tag attached by a wire. The tag was being blown by the wind, and with each swing, it rapped against the metal pole. This was the source of the mysterious tapping sound he had heard.

Surrounding the pole were numerous holes, each one six inches across and perfectly round.

Davidge dropped to his knees to finger the holes, unbelievingly. "Core samples," he whispered. "Goddamn, fucking core samples!"

He stood up again and stared into the sky. Where were they? Were they coming back? He peered at the metal tag. Who was Ackerman? And what did 4S-J mean? Was this a dry, abandoned exploration, or . . . ?

Beyond the pole was a mound, partially hidden in the steam. Davidge dropped the tag and crossed to it slowly. It was only more litter—beer cans, faded papers, all manner of items used and discarded. A garbage heap.

There were bugs and worms crawling in the mess, some things that looked like millipedes and others that looked like scorpions. Davidge was about to back away in disgust when something else caught his eyes, something white. Gingerly, he pushed aside some of the garbage and reached for it—

Two huge, empty eye sockets stared back at him.

The skull had a high, smooth brow. The lower jaw was missing, but the upper half of the turtle-like beak was evident. The center of the forehead—was marked by a round rough hole, just big enough for Davidge to put his finger through.

It was the skull of a Drac, killed by a bullet through the brain.

25

SOFT FLURRIES OF SNOW were drifting down through the air, not cold enough to sting yet, but cold enough to chill.

The ground was already hard and frosty. Davidge's footsteps crunched through the dead leaves and other debris on the forest floor. The trees above wore icy fringes.

Davidge started calling for Jerry as soon as he was close enough, but as he approached, he saw that the hut looked deserted. There was no smoke coming from the fire. Davidge's heart popped; for a single sickening moment, he was terrifed that—

He charged for the hut, shouting as he ran, "Jerry! Jeerrryy!" His feet pounded across the ground, sending wet sprays in all directions.

And then the Drac came heavily out of the shelter and stood up to face him. The Drac didn't look well. It looked *swollen.*

Davidge stopped short. He wanted to run to Jerry and hug the goddamn lizard, but—instead he stopped and looked. "Jerry? I didn't see any smoke and I thought..."

"You thought I had died perhaps? Without waiting for you?" The Drac hissed and smirked, but only half-heartedly. "I would not give you the pleasure of my death just yet, ugly *Irkmann.*"

"Well, I'm glad to hear that. Because I wanted to see your face again."

"My face? Why?"

"I wanted to see what it would do when I did this."
Davidge abruptly sang a quick phrase from the *Talman*.

Jerry's eyes widened in surprise.

Davidge kept singing, all the way through to the end
of the verse.

"The path of the wanderer has only one end," translated the Drac, "—for there is really only one journey;
it is both common and unique. Every journey is both
same and different, and every journey ends where it
began: in everything and nothing. The only choice is
what we see along the way, what we learn from it, and
who we teach it to."

Jerry's eyes were bright. It added, "You sing it well
. . . even for an *Irkmann*."

Davidge nodded his appreciation. Somehow the mere
words "Thank you," would not be enough. "You are a
good teacher, Jerry," he managed to say.

Jerry shook its head. "The student does the work. The
teacher merely sets the table." Abruptly, it said, "You
must build a fire, Willy. I am cold."

"Oh God, of course. Come on, let's get inside." He
followed the Drac back into the shelter. "How long has
the fire been out?"

"Three days."

"And you couldn't build a new one?"

"I—was not—able to gather wood."

Davidge looked around the shelter. It was in complete
disarray, as if someone had been raging . . . or delirious.
There was a smell of illness in the hut and the stack of
firewood had been badly depleted.

"It's going to take some time, Drac. I'll have to go
out for wood and then we'll have to dry it out. Here,
put on my coat, it'll keep you warm. I won't be long."

The Drac did not protest. It wrapped itself in Davidge's heavy cuca-skin coat and then wrapped its own

cuca-skin blanket around that. "I am glad you came back," it said. "Davidge—how cold do you think it is going to get?"

"I don't know, Jerry. I guess we'll find out." Davidge still didn't move to go looking for wood. "Jerry, what's wrong?"

The Drac looked at him. "Nothing is wrong. Everything is happening the way it is supposed to happen. It is just goddamned inconvenient, that is all."

"What is—?"

"I could not go with you," said the Drac, "because it is no longer my life alone that I am in charge of. I am not fat. I am not lazy. Davidge..." The Drac hesitated, looking for a word, "I am waiting a new life. A kid." It pantomimed. "A small person?"

"Huh?" Davidge heard the words, but not the meaning.

The Drac slowly straightened. Its belly protruded forward in a delicate curve. Davidge suddenly understood.

"Oh, Jesus! Are you telling me that you're...? Pregnant? A baby?"

The Drac nodded.

"Oh, Jesus Christ!" Davidge didn't know whether to laugh or shout or offer congratulations or what—and then he realized how serious a matter it really was. He said, "But how? Who—? Don't you look at me like that! This is one bastard I'm *not* responsible for!"

"No," said Jerry, stonily. "This bastard is mine."

"But, Jerry, you can't! I mean, not *here!* We're not ...We don't...I don't...This is crazy!"

"I told you I was not sane, ugly *Irkmann*. You did not understand then. You do not understand now. It is the season. It is my time. With you humans, a new birth is something you choose to create. With Dracs, it comes with the season for birthing. It happens when it happens.

Perhaps you have not read the verse yet about the parent and the child?"

"I read it. I didn't understand it. It was something I was going to ask you about."

"Well, now you don't have to ask. You will learn it like a Drac."

"Shit!" said Davidge, mostly to himself. "I'm sorry, Jerry. This is the one thing I didn't expect. I don't know how to deal with this, on top of everything else."

Jerry frowned at him. "On top of everything else? What did you find, Willy?"

"Nothing. Nothing at all." Davidge shivered. "I'd better go get some wood." He left the hut in a hurry, so Jerry wouldn't see what a lousy liar he was.

26

THE WINTER HIT WITH A VENGEANCE. The wind swept through the forest with hurricane brutality, driving great walls of ice and sleet before it. The trees groaned under the onslaught. Branches cracked under pressure, dropping sudden avalanches of snow on the forest floor.

Their tiny shelter had almost disappeared under the snow; it was a frozen mound, with only a stream of smoke rising from a hole at the top.

The temperatures were dropping alarmingly.

Davidge had packed the walls of the shelter with the blue moss from the trees. It made a wonderful insulator and it even worked a little bit like an air freshener, giving off a faint, spicy smell. Bits of the moss, when dried out, could be used to start a fire. If there was firewood.

But it wasn't enough.

Davidge had to scrounge farther and farther every day for fallen limbs, and when the wind howled like this, he didn't dare leave the shelter for fear of not being able to find his way back again. It was almost as loud as the meteor shower.

Inside, however, there was respite.

There was even time to study.

Davidge lowered the *Talman* and looked across at Jerry. The Drac was sewing a small garment out of cuca-skin. For a moment, Davidge admired the simple pastoral elegance of the act—it was a Drac sewing a baby garment out of Mock Turtle hide, and it was beautiful.

"*Kos son dedu*, Jerry?"

"*Shalpu g'dla Zammis.*"

"*Zammis?*" Davidge asked.

Jerry put one hand on its swollen midsection. "*Ae. Zammis.*"

"*Koda miy zhdhom da Zammis?*"

"Soon," smiled Jerry.

Davidge nodded. He started to toss another piece of wood onto the fire. Instead, he just stirred up the embers and put the piece of wood aside. Not yet.

"It is cold, Willy." Jerry noticed what he was doing. "And the wood is for burning."

"Jerry, I'm worried that there won't be enough."

"Read Chapter 42, Verse 69."

"No." Davidge put the *Talman* down and looked across to Jerry. "This is not about what I'm feeling inside. This is about our lack of firewood. This storm might go for two or three days. I don't think we have enough wood to last."

"Chapter 42, Verse 69. Translate it, please."

Davidge reopened the *Talman* and found his place. "If you do not believe in miracles, you will not recognize them when they happen around you. If you do believe in miracles, you will see them everywhere, every day."

Jerry nodded. "Go on. What does it say next?"

Davidge sighed. "Therefore, the person who is able to see the bountifulness of the universe can not only expect a miracle; that person can depend on them." Davidge closed the book. "Jerry, that's all very well and good—but I don't see how that's going to put wood on the fire."

"It won't," said Jerry. "You will."

"And where the hell am I going to find it?" As if to

underline his thought, the shelter shook again under the onslaught of the wind. Outside, the trees groaned. "If I go out in that storm now, I'd be lost in minutes, if I didn't freeze to death first."

The Drac looked up and smiled. "Is the trouble with you, ugly *Irkmann,* is that you have no willingness to wait. When it is time for *aelova,* then *aelova* happens. And not before. And not simply because ugly *Irkmann* demands it."

Davidge felt frustrated. "Okay. Maybe I'm having a semantic problem here, Jerry. Maybe miracle isn't the right word. To me, a miracle is something that happens without reason or obvious cause—something very lucky. What does the *Talman* mean by *aelova?*"

Jerry frowned at the stitch it was working on, then said, *"Aelova* is any happening that makes your life work better. It is not event as much as it is . . . opportunity. It is up to observer to turn opportunity into event. Miracles happen to those who are willing to create them. I think that is correct. It is as close as I can say."

"Never mind. I *gavey.*" Davidge huddled in his coat. "But I'm not going to believe in either miracles or *aelovas* until somebody drops a load of firewood at our front door."

"Be careful what you wish for, ugly *Irkmann.* Remember, the universe is a practical joker. It put you here to be the . . . fairy godmother of my child."

"Please. Don't remind me."

Just outside the hut, there was a sudden crackling sound, and something huge began to groan—

"What the—?"

The noise grew suddenly louder and closer. The groaning abruptly became a scream of ripping wood—and then the whole shelter reverberated with a sudden thunderous crash!

Both Jerry and Davidge leapt to their feet. Davidge was the first one out the door. He just stopped and stared. Jerry came out right behind him, sheltering itself against the wind.

A tree had fallen.

Not just a tree, but one of the great Grandfather Banyans. Its brittle branches had broken off, scattering and flying in all directions. There were pieces of wood everywhere. The wind howled hysterically through the forest of firewood, hurling mocking flurries of snow into Davidge's face.

"Your firewood is here," said Jerry.

Davidge turned and looked at the Drac. "I don't know how you did it, you goddamn lizard, but I'm impressed as hell at the lengths you will go to convince me." He poked Jerry's shoulder. "Come on, get back inside. You'll freeze your smallberries off. If you have any. Which I doubt."

Jerry returned to its sewing as Davidge piled the last of their wood on the fire. The shelter was going to be warm again! "I told you to be careful what you wish for, ugly *Irkmann*. Now, perhaps, you will believe me, no?"

"Now, perhaps I will believe, no," said Davidge. "But at least I'll expect."

27

THE STORM LET UP LATER in the day, long enough for Davidge to bring in enough wood to last them for a week, if necessary. And—just to be on the safe side—he dragged two of the larger limbs over to the side of the hut where he could get to them easily, if need be.

Fortunately, they had water, and they had dried meat and tubers. And they even still had some of Jerry's god-awful ration bars.

They would survive a while longer.

Davidge came back into the hut and began building up the fire for the night. "Now, I won't have to huddle up next to a goddamn lizard for warmth," he said.

But that night, when it came time for sleep, he lay his bed next to the Drac's again. The two of them settled down together, pulling the cuca-skins warmly over them. Davidge curled up comfortably behind the Drac, even putting one arm protectively around his friend.

"I thought you said you wouldn't have to huddle up next to a goddamn lizard anymore," said Jerry.

"I told the truth," grunted Davidge. "I said I wouldn't have to huddle up next to a goddamn lizard for the warmth."

"Oh," said Jerry.

They lay there for a while together, neither one sleeping yet. Finally, Davidge asked, "Jerry?"

"Yes, Willy."

"Can I ask you a question?"

"What?"

"Do Dracs . . . have lovers?"

"Nae gavey. What is 'lovers?'"

"Um, well . . . you know that it takes two human beings to make a baby—right?—a man and a woman. Well, that's lovers. A man and a woman. But Dracs have only one sex, right?"

"Is right."

"So. What I'm getting at is . . . " Davidge felt acutely embarrassed; he wished he hadn't brought the subject up now. But he pushed on anyway. "Do Dracs get married? Or what?"

"I don't understand. What is 'married?'"

"Well, when a man and a woman love each other, when they *choose* each other, they make a . . . an agreement to be a family. That agreement is called a marriage. There's a whole ceremony. Then, after a while, if they want to, they start making babies. And that's how they enlarge the family. But a family always starts with two lovers."

"We live together," said the Drac, puzzled. "And soon, we shall have *Zammis.* Is this what you are asking? That we are lovers?"

"Um, no. Um. What I'm trying to ask . . . " Davidge leveled himself up on one elbow, frowning.

Jerry turned on its back to look over at him. "You are having trouble finding the words?"

"No. I am having trouble finding the courage. If I'm asking something embarrassing, I apologize in advance. But—I mean 'lovers'—in the *physical* sense."

"Lovers in the physical sense," the Drac repeated, uncomprehendingly. "I am sorry, Willy. *Nae gavey.*"

"Um, okay." Davidge swallowed hard. "What I'm trying to ask is when—or how—do Dracs have sex? Or do Dracs even have sex?"

"Have sex?"

"Make love. Mate. Um . . . Exchange genetic material?" Davidge felt like an idiot.

Jerry frowned. "Exchange genetic material?" It turned the words over and over, considering what Davidge had asked. And then it realized, and started giggling—a silly, high-pitched, hissing, sputtering sound.

Davidge started to roll away, but Jerry reached out with one hand and touched his forearm. "I am not laughing at you, Willy. I am laughing at our differences. I make assumptions. You make assumptions. We are both stupid." Jerry turned to look at Davidge. "Dracs have ceremonies for mating, a celebration of parent and child and unborn generation. It is very beautiful. It is where children are taught to exchange genetic material to strengthen the next generation. So, yes, Dracs mate. But, no, not like *Irkmann*. Dracs do not make lovers to make families. Drac families are based on line of parent."

Davidge nodded. "So, Dracs don't have lovers at all?"

"Nae."

"Oh," said Davidge. He lay down again, but he didn't put his arm back around Jerry.

He couldn't imagine it.

It sounded so *lonely*.

But the Drac had accepted it as just the way things were.

Davidge didn't even know what question to ask next. What did the Dracs do instead of taking lovers? What did they do for relationships?

If the Dracs didn't take permanent mates, then clearly the pair-bond relationship simply didn't exist for them. And that implied that the only bonding relationship that a Drac would have in its whole life would be as child-to-parent or parent-to-child.

And that meant—

Davidge lay there wondering about the assumptions he had made—the ones he still hadn't realized. Had he been operating under some assumption that would kill them both?

Damn! I've been stupid!

He'd been thinking that Jerry *felt* something for him. Underneath all that 'ugly *Irkmann*' and 'goddamn lizard' bullshit, he'd been assuming that there was . . . he'd thought that Jerry *cared*.

But now, he knew that the lizard was incapable of that emotion. The goddamn lizard didn't care, because it didn't know how to care. It *couldn't* care.

Damn, that hurt.

Never mind. It was better to discover it now. Instead of later, when—

Davidge knew he had to stop thinking of Jerry as a human being in a lizard suit. Despite their similarities, the Drac was still an alien being. All the similarities between them merely served to distract him from their differences.

The Drac wasn't mammal. It didn't have the same relationship with its parents. Parent. Singular. It wouldn't have the same relationship with its child. The Dracs were lizards. They didn't pair bond. They didn't have lovers. They didn't have friends. And that meant . . . they didn't have loyalty either.

And . . . if it came down to it, if it were a matter of survival, the Drac would have to choose its child over Davidge. It would have to. That's the way its machinery was wired up.

Davidge had been deluding himself. He'd been feeling . . . fatherly.

No. That wasn't it. He'd been feeling—in love.

Damn stupid ugly *Irkmann,* he told himself. That's how desperate and horny and lonely you really are! Even a Drac is starting to look good!

He curled up with his back to Jerry. They lay in silence, back to back. Jerry's soft even breathing told Davidge that the Drac had already fallen asleep. The goddamn lizard.

Damn it to hell!

28

DAVIDGE HAD NEVER THOUGHT of Jerry as a restless sleeper, but tonight Jerry was certainly doing a lot of thrashing around.

Davidge rolled over, away from the Drac, rolling his blanket tighter around himself. "Mmmmhhmmmmmpphff."

The Drac kicked him.

"Aww, come on, Jerry. Let me sleep, will ya?"

The Drac was still thrashing. It kicked him again.

"Will you stop—?" Davidge rolled over—

—the Drac was struggling with something long and pink.

Jerry's eyes were bulging. Its mouth was caught in a soundless scream. Its body was being dragged toward a newly formed pit at one side of the hut: It was trying desperately to kick loose.

"Oh, shit!" Davidge dove for the gun. There wasn't time; the jaws of the predator were already opening to engulf the helpless Drac.

Without hesitating, Davidge grabbed a handful of red hot coals from the fire and shoved them into the monster's gullet.

The creature screamed—choked and screamed—it gurgled and smoked and came slithering out of the hole; ten feet long, pink and hairless! It writhed and snapped in agony, flailing its tail around, smashing the fire and filling the room with flying embers. It flung the Drac sideways against one wall.

Davidge grabbed at Jerry and pulled! The hut was filling with smoke. He crawled for the door, pulling the limp Drac behind him. "Come on, Jerry!"

And then, abruptly, they were outside in the glare of dawn and crawling through the snow. Davidge was coughing; Jerry was still gasping and choking. Davidge stood up, pulled Jerry to its feet and ran, pulling the Drac with him.

The gale-force winds pulled them apart. "Jerry!" Davidge turned around and around in confusion.

Inside the shelter, the mortally wounded predator screamed and lashed out in all directions, smashing into the walls of the shelter, sending fireworks of flying embers into the freezing air.

As if in answer, the forest cracked and groaned ominously under the onslaught of the wind.

"Jerry!" Davidge screamed.

There it was, staggering blindly. Davidge struggled toward the Drac.

Something *cracked*. Davidge leapt, pulling Jerry with him. The tree screamed as it toppled—its great branches sweeping downward, tangling and pulling at the trees around it. Davidge pulled Jerry backward, away. The tree thundered into the ground with a bone-rattling *thud*.

But the crackling noise of its collapse was continuing! Davidge whirled—a second tree was falling. The first one had pulled it loose. Massive and knotted, it arced over, slowly at first, then faster and faster until it came down with a crashing jar—right on top of their cuca shelter, exploding it into fragments and choking off the predator's high shrill screams.

Then nothing. Only the desperate howling of the wind.

They sank to the ground together, next to one of the

fallen trees. Davidge took the Drac's face in his hands and lifted it, looking at Jerry's lacerated neck. It was bad. The Drac pulled his hands down from its face and looked at Davidge's palms.

They were blistered and burned.

Davidge looked at his hands, he looked at Jerry's face, he looked back at the shelter, and all he could feel was the crushing weight of his own despair. Everything. Everything was lost, just like that. The tears came flooding to his eyes. "I'm sorry, Jerry." He realized he was bawling like a baby and he didn't care. "I give up. That's it. I know when I'm licked."

Jerry didn't speak. It just stared at Davidge, waiting for the fit to pass. It had never seen the Earthman like this before. Around them, the rotted trees groaned before the wind. Jerry looked up at them and listened to their noises.

"Willy! We must get out of the forest."

"I can't. What's the use?"

"Come on, Willy!" The Drac was insistent. "We will be killed here." Jerry stood up, it started pulling Davidge to his feet.

Davidge refused to rise. "Good! I'm tired of living!"

"Then you are a fucking asshole!"

Davidge came up swinging—caught himself, stopped and stared at Jerry.

"Come," said the Drac. "You and I. We must not go to waste!"

They staggered back to the shelter and picked quickly through the rubble. The storm was howling. Jerry found a water bag. Davidge found a bundle of smoked meat. Jerry found a knife. Davidge found bundle of metal fragments that he called his "tool kit" and the baby clothes for Zammis. Jerry grabbed a cuca-skin blanket and improvised a bundle.

In the distance, a tree collapsed and crashed to the forest floor.

Davidge looked up long enough to remark, "So. It does make noise when a tree falls in the forest. I know a lot of people will be glad to hear that."

Jerry was staring at him.

"You want to go?" said Davidge. "Okay, let's go. Let's go *now!*"

He started trudging through the snow. Jerry hurried to catch up to him.

The wind was rising.

29

SOMEHOW, THEY MADE IT THROUGH THE STORM. Somehow, they made it through the Dead Forest. The wind smashed into them; they had to lean into it to walk. They staggered from tree to tree, lest the wind blow them down. The sleet blinded their eyes and filled their mouths. All around them, the branches cracked and the trees groaned under the strain. Ancient limbs crashed to the ground. In the distance trees were toppling. The forest roared with the noise.

And yet, somehow, they made it through.

"'This is how you know if your job is done,'" Jerry quoted from the *Talman*. "'If you're still alive, it isn't.'" And dragged Davidge after. "Come, Willy. There is still work to do."

They walked for what must have been hours. The day grew brighter, but the storm never abated. It swept across the rocks and the craters and shrieked as if its belly were being ripped out. Davidge's face hurt. His hands and his feet were numb. But he wouldn't quit. If the goddamn lizard wanted to walk, he'd walk. He put one foot in front of the other and kept on going.

They came out on a rocky area, stark and barren. Jagged black outcroppings thrust up through the blanket of snow and ice. The wind scraped across the top of the world, catching its breath for a new assault.

Davidge and Jerry stumbled on, frostbitten and snow-blind. They climbed, wedging their hands and feet into cracks in the ice, pulling each other up one at a time. They were crawling blindly now. Davidge knew it. He didn't know where they were anymore. Probably the Drac didn't either. It didn't matter. They had to keep moving. He didn't remember why.

They reached a ledge where they were sheltered from the wind, and the Drac collapsed in a heap.

"This iss as far as I go, Willy."

"The hell you say! The cold will kill us if we stop."

"I can't!"

"Bullshit! It was your fucking idea to move!"

"Leave me alone, Willy!"

Davidge crawled over to the Drac. He grabbed Jerry, hard, and wrapped their single blanket around the two of them. He held Jerry as close to him as he could. "I don't care if you are a goddamn lizard," he screamed to be heard over the wind, "if I have to live, so do you! You're all I have and I'm not gonna fucking lose you!"

"Willy!" the Drac was gasping. "Willy, stop! I hurrt."

"Good! It means you're still alive!"

"Willy! Please!"

"Talk to me, goddamnit! Keep moving! Keep talking!" He pulled the Drac to its feet and shoved it forward. "Come on! Tell me about Zammis. I want to know about Zammis!"

"What?" gasped Jerry. "What can I tell you?"

"Tell me about the name!" Davidge staggered. "Why did you call it Zammis?"

"Why—?"

"Yeah! *Why?*"

"Because that is its name, stupid *Irkmann!*"

"Yeah, but why! Keep talking, you goddamned lizard. What does the name mean?"

The Drac didn't answer at first; it was negotiating its way past a rocky shelf.

"What does the name mean?" repeated Davidge.

"Nae gavey!" screamed Jerry. "It doesn't mean anything yet. It's just the *next* name."

"Next name?" Davidge followed the Drac past the rocky shelf. They were both screaming at each other now.

"Yes! You stupid, goddamned, ugly *Irkmann!* Do you know nothing? There are only five names in a Drac family! I am of the *Jeriba* family. We are—" the Drac stumbled in the snow. Davidge pulled it to its feet and they stumbled on together. Jerry continued, "We are very noble. I am Shigan. Before me was my parent, Gothig. Before Gothig was Haesni. Before Haesni was Ty. Before Ty was Zammis. And before Zammis was Shigan." The Drac caught a faceful of snow and coughed.

Davidge helped Jerry wipe away the snow, then shouted, "Why only five names? Humans have thousands of names!"

"The names mean nothing!" Jerry shouted back. "It is the deeds that must be remembered. I can recite the history of my line back to the founding of my planet by Jeriba Ty one hundred and seventy-nine generations ago. One day I will stand with Jeriba Zammis before the Holy Council of Elders in the High Halls of Draco and recite our line, so that Zammis may join the society and faith of all Dracs."

"Yeah, not if you quit." Davidge gave the Drac a rough shove forward.

"Who is quitting, *Irkmann?* Who is quitting?"

Davidge laughed loudly.

"What is so funny?"

"We are!" Davidge tried to explain. "What a pair we are! We deserve each other! We're each too fucking mean to let the other one die!"

═══════ 30

MIRACLES, THOUGHT DAVIDGE; *expect a miracle.*

Depend on it.

And boy, do we need one now!

Okay, God or *Shizumaat* or whoever you are, Davidge said to himself, now's the time. Do your stuff.

Davidge bumped into Jerry, nearly knocking the Drac forward into the snow. He reached and grabbed. "What is it? Why'd you stop?"

Jerry pointed ahead, then turned and pounded Davidge madly on the back. Davidge stared forward—at a dark opening, gaping in the snowbound rock.

A cave!

They stumbled forward. For half a moment, Davidge worried about hibernating grizzlies, then said, "The hell with it! I don't make faulty miracles!" and stumbled after Jerry.

The inside of the cave was huge. It had a high, naturally vaulted ceiling. Large snowdunes and icicles were accumulated below openings in the ceiling. *Good!* thought Davidge. *There's ventilation!*

Jerry was standing, stopped at a loss. It turned around and looked at Davidge.

"Come here," said the Earthman. He stepped over to the Drac and took its bundle from it. He led Jerry up to the highest, warmest part of the cave he could find and dumped their few pitiful belongings onto the ground, then spread the blanket out as a bed. Quickly, he pulled off his coat and the Drac's too. "Lie down," he ordered.

The Drac did so, shivering. Davidge lay down next to the Drac, wrapping the two of them in both of their coats and then the blanket around that. It might work. He wrapped his naked arms and legs around Jerry's body, hoping that their shared warmth would be enough to keep them both from freezing to death.

To hell with it! thought Davidge. *I can care enough for both of us!* He cradled himself carefully around Jerry, and using the knuckles of his burned hands, began to slowly rub the warmth back into Jerry's arms and legs.

Jerry shivered within itself for a moment, then slowly, put its arms around Davidge and held on tight.

"Jerry—?"

"Shh, ugly *Irkmann*."

"Okay . . . goddamn lizard."

They fell asleep that way, wrapped up in each other's arms and legs and blankets.

The wind howled anew, but it couldn't reach them inside the cave, and after a while, it gave up and went away.

31

DAVIDGE WOKE UP FIRST. His hands were hurting. That was a good sign; it meant he was healing. It meant he was still alive.

He rolled away from Jerry so he could look at his hands. They were scabbed and crusted. He tried flexing them gently. They weren't as bad as they looked. Good.

He sat up, pulling the topmost coat up around his shoulders. Jerry woke up then and rolled over to look at him. "Davidge, you sleep with lizards."

Davidge grinned. "And you snore like a chain saw." He shivered at the bite in the morning air—outside the wind was howling like a pack of lawyers. Davidge shivered and scrunched back down beneath the blankets. He put his arms around the Drac again. "Are you warm enough?"

Jerry nodded.

"Good."

After a moment, Jerry asked, "Willy?"

"Yes, Jerry?"

"This . . . holding. This is how humans . . . What is the word? . . . make love?"

"It's part of it, yes," Davidge admitted.

"Oh," said Jerry.

"Do you want me to *not* hold you?"

"No," said Jerry. "I don't mind. It helps keep me warm."

"Good," said Davidge.

After another moment, Jerry asked, "Willy?"

"Yes, Jerry?"

"Do you like this . . . holding?"

Davidge admitted it with a nod. "Yes."

"Why?"

Davidge was silent for a moment. "Because . . . it helps keep me warm too."

"Liar," said the Drac.

"But it's true."

"You said you would not have to huddle against a lizard again for warmth."

"That was when we had firewood."

"But you huddled anyway. So, you lied then. And you lie now, right?"

"Okay, so what?"

"So, I want to *gavey*. Why does ugly *Irkmann* like to huddle with goddamn lizard?"

"Because . . . it's a way of demonstrating that I . . . care about you."

"Oh." And then, "I thought so."

"It's called a hug," said Davidge.

"A hug. Yes." The lizard fell silent.

Davidge couldn't stand it. "Jerry?" he asked.

"Yes, Willy?"

"Do lizards . . . care?"

"Don't be stupid. A Drac family is built on the caring for life."

"No, I mean—do Dracs care about other Dracs at all? Or is it only family?"

"Oh," said Jerry, understanding the question. "Oh," it said again, as it understood the question *behind* the question. "I see."

"No," said Davidge. "No, forget it."

"I cannot forget it. You have asked it. It is in my

head. Your question implies . . . that a person is incomplete without a coupling. *Irkmenn* need this coupling to be complete?"

"Yeah," Davidge admitted.

Jerry was silent.

"Dracs are complete then?" Davidge asked. "By themselves."

"Yes," said Jerry.

"Mm," said Davidge. "It sounds lonely."

The Drac shrugged. "Lonely. I cannot imagine lonely."

Davidge sniffed. "You have to have a soul first." He regretted the remark instantly.

But Jerry wasn't offended. The Drac simply snorted. "A soul is an *Irkmann* concept."

"So? Do Dracs have souls?"

"That question can only be asked in Engleesh, Willy. If you ask it in Drac, it is not a question. It is like asking, 'Why is the sky?'"

"Why is the sky? Is there an answer to that?"

"Oh, sure—" giggled Jerry. "'Why not?'"

"That's *bad.*" Davidge poked the Drac playfully in the ribs. "Okay, I've got one for you. What is the sound of one hand clapping?"

"Ah! Iss good! Iss another one from Mickey Mooze?"

"Yeah. One of his best."

"I will ponder it," said Jerry. "But to return to your other question, ugly *Irkmann,* the question of what is a soul. Your answer can be found by studying the *Talman.* The answers to everything are found in the study of the *Talman.*"

"Huh? Now, wait a minute! The *Talman* has no answers at all in it. It's almost all about questions!"

"That's very good, Willy. Very good. The secret to finding the answer lies in asking the right question. If you ask the right question, the answer takes care of itself.

That's why the *Talman* is mostly about how to ask questions."

"Mm," said Davidge.

"You have been asking wrong questions, my friend?"

"I don't know," said Davidge. "I do know I haven't asked the right one yet." He sat up abruptly. "Are you hungry?"

"We have food?" Jerry asked.

"Mm hm." Davidge reached over and snagged the bag of dried meat. He passed Jerry a slice of cuca and took one for himself. "You know, maybe we could open up a little place here. You could frighten the customers and I could ruin the food."

The Drac didn't answer; it was sniffing at the meat, but it stopped as a wave of pain shuddered through its body. Jerry lowered the meat to its lap and clutched at its side. There was a sadness in its eyes.

Abruptly, Jerry said, "Let me teach you the Jeriba line."

"Before or after breakfast?"

Jerry stiffened. "This is an honor, Willy."

"I'm sorry, Jerry, but right now, just staying alive is going to be honor enough."

"All right. Then I will learn *your* lineage. Let us begin with your parent. Who was he?"

"They. It takes two, remember?"

"Right. Who were they?"

Davidge shrugged. He said, around a mouthful of meat, "Dad's name is Carl. My mother is Edna."

"And their deeds?"

"Deeds. Um—" Davidge chewed thoughtfully. "Well, Dad works for a company that makes ultra-large-scale wafer electronics, and Mom used to be a residential therapist before she got married."

"What is a residential therapist?"

"A kind of a nurse."

"Good." Jerry nodded. "And who were their parents?"

"Oh, well, we used to visit Grandpa when I was just a kid. He had a place in the country. I guess he was a farmer. Nana was a good cook. That's all I remember."

"And before them?"

Davidge scratched his head. "I think the family came over from England or Scotland originally."

"Ah, then that is your lineage. 'Here stands before you Willis E. Davidge, fighter pilot, son of Edna who used to be a therapist and Carl, maker of electronics, who in their time were born of Grandpa, possibly a farmer, and Nana, a good cook, descended from those who came from England or Scotland.'"

"You make it sound pretty thin."

Jerry shrugged. "Every line must start somewhere. I am honored that you have entrusted it to me." Jerry winced again. "Willy, please learn my lineage." It covered its pain and added, "Allow me to do you this honor. It will be an exchange of gifts between us."

Davidge sighed. "I don't feel very honorable, right now."

"No matter," said Jerry, and started singing: *"Son ich stayu, kos va Shigan, chamy'a de Jeriba, yaziki nech lich isnam liba, drazyor, par nuzhda...."*

32

THE STORM HOWLED for two days more, then abruptly, almost as suddenly as it had come, the wind died away.

Davidge stood at the mouth of the cave, his hands shoved deep into his pockets. Just how far was it back to their old camp anyway? There should still be salvageable things there. Maybe even the rest of their store of food.

No, they had food. The first order of priority had to be a fire.

So the real question was: How far was it back to the forest?

Wood shouldn't be a problem. The way the wind had been howling for the past three days, Davidge would be surprised if any trees at all were still standing in the Dead Forest.

It could be a long way to haul it though.

But he had his knife, and if he could find some of the purple vine, he could tie up a bundle and drag it up to the cave. That might work.

It did.

The Dead Forest was twice as far as Davidge thought, and the job of finding enough wood and tying it into a bundle took three times as long as Davidge expected.

But they would have fire.

And fire meant survival.

Davidge practiced reciting the Jeriba lineage all the

way down to the Dead Forest and then all the way back up to the cave with one bundle of wood on his back and a second one dragging through the snow behind him. He did this for three days in a row, until the wind started rising again and the storm resumed its incessant howling.

He found Jerry curled up near the fire, its eyes narrowed in pain. The Drac's belly was distended enormously.

"Jerry—?"

The Drac looked up sadly. "Today must be... Wednesday."

"Huh? What are you talking about."

"Anything can happen. Zammis is coming."

"Are you sure?"

"I am as sure as you are ugly."

"I'm sorry," Davidge said, realizing the stupidity of his remark. He squatted down next to Jerry and offered the Drac a drink of water.

"Thank you."

"What should I do?"

"I don't know," said Jerry. "I think that something is wrong."

Davidge put his hand on Jerry's forehead. It was something to do. He said, "You'll be all right. Women always get nervous before labor."

"I am not a woman," said Jerry.

"Yeah, well, pregnant people—things—get nervous. Everybody gets nervous before labor."

"I am not nervous either. Something is wrong." The Drac winced abruptly.

"Jerry!"

The Drac opened its eyes again. "I am not going anywhere, *Irkmann*."

"Better not. I can't run this place by myself."

"You do not like being alone, do you, Willy?"

"I can handle it."

"No, I said it wrong. I meant your species. Humans do not like being alone. Humans need partners. This iss correct?"

"Yeah, this is correct."

"I am sorry for you," said the Drac. "It sseemss a terribly crippled way to exist. Never complete except when you are exchanging genetic material." Jerry winced again. "I am sorry I could not be more of a partner for you." Jerry closed its eyes and concentrated on its breathing.

"Jerry!"

The wave of pain passed and Drac opened its eyes for a brief moment. "Poor ugly *Irkmann*. You will be lonely without your old enemy, eh?" It closed its eyes again.

Davidge knelt beside Jerry. He soaked a piece of rag in some melted snow and put it on the Drac's forehead. "Jerry, don't talk like that."

"I think—" said the Drac. "I think that Zammis is in the wrong position. If we can move it . . . maybe . . ." Jerry started tugging at its coat, but it was too weak to move.

Davidge began to unlace the Drac's cuca skin jacket. As it pulled away from the Drac's body he saw for the first time Jerry's enormous swollen belly. Across the surface of this mound ran a cleft. It looked like a ragged inflamed wound held together by inner tendons.

"Push me over on my side, Willy."

Davidge started to do so. The Drac gasped in pain. Davidge hesitated—

"Do it, Willy! On my side. There. Can you see it?"

A round lump was pushing up on one side of the Drac's belly.

"Yes."

"Then push on it. We must turn Zammis around."

Davidge put his hands gingerly on the lump. He pushed tentatively.

"Push harder! Harder!"

The Drac's skin was hot. Davidge pushed. The lump moved. Jerry screamed, but its eyes were steady and coherent.

Abruptly, Jerry spoke. "Willy!"

"What?"

"Promise me. You will be a parent for Zammis."

"Hey! I told you not to talk like that."

"Willy! You must take my place. When the time comes, you must find the way to take Zammis home. You will stand beside Zammis before the Holy Council on Draco and recite its lineage. You must do this, Willy! Swear this to me! You will take Zammis to Draco."

"Shut up! And keep pushing, or whatever it is you do."

"You will take Zammis to Draco. *Swear it, Willy.*"

"No!"

"Swear it. Swear it!"

"No, goddammit! I won't give you permission to die."

"Fuck you! Slave-eater! Why do you think I have been teaching you everything?" The Drac screamed and shuddered in pain. *"Irkmann! I beg you!"*

"All right, Jerry—all right, I swear. I'll take Zammis to Draco. I'll recite the lineage. Just please don't die on me. Please!"

The Drac sighed. "Good. Now you must open me, Davidge."

"What?" He shook his head.

"Here, this place—" The Drac's hand moved weakly.

Davidge hesitated, then forced himself to reach for the cleft in the Drac's belly.

"You must do this, Willy. Use your stength! Don't be afraid."

Davidge tried to pry the fold of skin apart. The Drac screamed, a high-pitched hissing that left Davidge shaken and trembling. He threw himself back, staring in horror.

"Open me, Willy! You have sworn."

"I can't do it, Jerry. I can't!"

The Drac was insistent. Its words were inescapable. "Damn you, *Irkmann!* You have sworn! Is this *Irkmann* honor? You will say anything, but your words mean nothing? I curse your *Irkmann* honor!"

Davidge was paralyzed. The Drac's eyes were burning. "Jerry, I . . ."

The Drac reached one hand toward him. For a moment, the hand wavered in the air. Davidge clutched it in his own.

"Willy, you have sworn."

Its body arched in agony, rising halfway up off the ground.

Jerry convulsed—a horrible hissing rattle came from its throat—and then it fell still.

Davidge looked down at the hand he clutched in his own. "Oh, God—" he choked.

Only the Drac's belly moved, as the thing inside it struggled against its own dying.

"No, Jerry. Please . . ."

The struggles of the unborn Drac became greater. Jerry's belly convulsed; the body shook and gyrated as the thing inside raged.

Davidge stared in horror, unable to move. He watched. Zammis's movements were ebbing. It must be growing weaker. "No, Jerry, please don't leave me alone."

And then, something inside Davidge snapped and he was clawing frantically at the belly of the dead Drac, tearing into the fold, ripping it open.

A thick, clear liquid burst out, soaking Davidge—he turned aside to retch—then forced himself to turn back and reach into the warm body cavity. He pulled out the tiny Drac and held it up to stare at it. Zammis.

It wasn't breathing.

Davidge shook the little Drac gently. He wiped at its nose and mouth and shook it again.

"What do I do with you, monster?"

He cradled the infant in one arm and pried open its tiny mouth with one finger. He lowered his own mouth over it and blew gently into the creature's lungs. He did it again; a third time and a fourth. He lost count.

"Come on, you little fucker. Breathe for me!"

Zammis coughed. It choked and began to cry—a terrifying, almost human-like wail.

Its three-fingered hand clutched at Davidge. Clutched for its parent.

33

WILLIS E. DAVIDGE, HUMAN BEING. Fighter pilot. God-parent of monsters.

Shit.

The universe was run by practical jokers.

"Tell me again about miracles, Jerry!" Davidge groaned as he dropped the last goddamn rock on the goddamn lizard's grave.

He straightened up and wrapped his cuca coat warm around himself. He stood there shivering and stared at the mound of rocks. Already, the snow was piling up around it. The wind blew ice and sleet into his eyes.

Davidge wiped at his cheeks. "You deserve better than this, you son of a bitch. You goddamn lizard. Jesus fucking Christ, I'm going to miss you!" Davidge howled into the wind, a scream of rage and frustration and despair.

The wind howled back, equally defiant. Davidge turned his back to it. He didn't want to go back up to the cave. Not just yet.

The baby was crying. It sounded like a cat fight.

"You were supposed to be sleeping, monster," Davidge shouted at the cave. The baby's cries were pitiful.

"Jesus Christ, Jerry! You taught me all about the *Talman* and the goddamn line of Jeriba, didn't you. That was just terrific. But you never said a word about the care and feeding of baby Dracs. What am I supposed to do?" He stared at the grave. "I'm a human! You want me to raise my own goddamn enemies now? Taking care of you should have been enough punishment."

The baby's cries were getting louder and more insistent.

"Oh, shit." Davidge turned and headed for the cave.

Zammis stopped its crying as soon as it saw him. It was wrapped in Jerry's cuca coat. Its eyes were large and yellow. It stretched its arms out toward him. "Mewww-phhhhugh?" it asked.

"Oh, that's cute. Real cute. Well, it won't fucking work!"

But hell, it wasn't the baby's fault. The poor little lizard. Its luck was even worse than the ugly *Irkmann*'s.

"Dammit, Jerry!" Davidge shouted, momentarily scaring the baby Drac. "This is crazy. I can't!"

Yes, ugly Irkmann. That is how you argue for your limits.

Davidge felt his frustration building to a peak. Jerry had trained him too well. Even after he'd planted the goddamn lizard, he could still hear its side of the conversation. He knew how the lizard would answer each of his excuses.

"Meww-phhugh?" the baby asked again.

Go ahead, ugly Irkmann. Now, explain it to Zammis.

Davidge felt his throat constricting. He very nearly broke down. "Hey, little guy! I'm sorry. I just don't have any way of caring for you. Jesus! I just don't!"

Davidge knew what he had to do. And the sooner he got it over with, the better. He picked up a large boulder from the cave floor and raised it high over the baby's huddled form.

"Mewwwwphhhhhhugh!" wailed Zammis.

Crying out with anguish, Davidge turned and hurled the boulder against the opposite wall of the cave. It banged against the rock, bounced and rolled harmlessly away. He dropped to his knees and scooped the baby up. He opened his cuca-skin jacket and held Zammis against his skin for warmth. He made himself comfortable against one wall and began to rock the infant softly.

"Okay—it's okay, little guy, little monster. You just get warm now, okay? You just get warm."

Zammis gurgled.

"Yeah, that goes for me too. I hope you're not going to be too hard to housebreak. How do you housebreak a Drac anyway? Yeah, well, never mind."

The baby stopped crying at the sound of Davidge's voice. It clutched one tiny green hand around Davidge's finger. Its tiny claws were sharp.

"I'm sorry. I don't know any Drac lullabies. I can tell you a bedtime story, if you want. Once upon a time there was a great big ugly monster named Godzilla." Davidge shut up. The joke wasn't funny.

"I'll tell you what," Davidge said. "You might as well start learning your history now, monster." He closed his eyes and began to recite: *"Son ich stayu, kos va Shigan, chamy'a de Jeriba, yaziki nech lich isnam liba, drazyor, par nuzhda...."*

Only now there were one hundred and eighty verses.

By the time he finished, the baby was snoring softly.

"... and the last one in line was a goddamn lizard who left his best friend to raise his only child!" Davidge finished in a cold dry whisper; but there was no real anger in his voice.

The song had done its job. His rage had vanished.

In its place, there was only a huge empty Drac-shaped hole.

"Dammit, Jerry—" he choked, "—I miss you so much."

It was as if the last barrier had snapped.

The tears welled up in Davidge's eyes and he began to sob. He held the baby Drac as tightly as he could and let the tears flow long and hard. "Goddamn lizard. Goddamn lizard. Goddamn Drac, Mickey Mouse-loving lizard!"

Zammis gurgled softly in its sleep.

34

"THIS IS CRAZY," Davidge said to the baby Drac. "You know it and I know it. But just in case you don't know it, you want me to go over the reasons why this is crazy again?"

"Gurgle," said Zammis.

"Right. Well, first of all, your people and my people are at war. And second of all, I don't know nothin' about birthin' no Dracons. And third of all, me sitting here and holding you and hugging you like this—that could very possibly be considered aiding and abetting the enemy."

"Gur-gurgle," said Zammis.

"That's a good point too," replied Davidge. "But I don't think the fact that you're a civilian is going to change matters much. I am going to have a hard time explaining you to my parents—and you are certainly going to have a hard time explaining me to your grandparent. Okay, let's try eating again. Right?"

Davidge bit off and began to chew a small piece of cuca meat. He chewed it until it was almost liquid, then took it out of his mouth and shoved the piece gently into the baby's mouth.

"Gugk," said Zammis.

"You're right. That's how I feel about it too, monster, but I cannot run down to my local market for a jar of Gerber's. It just ain't there, little guy. This is it. This is all there is."

Zammis blinked up at Davidge. Its mouth was pursed around the unfamiliar object.

"It's for eating."

"Gug-guk?"

"Right again. You're a smart little monster. I'll tell you something else. I am told that this is how eskimoes feed baby eskimoes, so maybe it'll work for baby monsters too."

Zammis' mouth started to work on the bit of meat. The baby swallowed the food abruptly and looked to Davidge for more.

"Well, I'll be—the son of an *Irkmann*," said Davidge.

"Gurk?" said Zammis, opening its mouth wide, like a baby bird.

"Attaboy. Well, okay!" Davidge began chewing a second piece of meat. He poked it quickly into the baby's gullet, not sure yet if Zammis could tell the difference between food and finger. "Eat that up and you'll grow up to be big and strong just like your—just like your parent. And then you can go out and kill ugly *Irkmenn* too."

"Glurk?"

"Mm hm. Wait a minute, it's still in the blender," said Davidge, chewing. He poked the third piece of food into the baby's mouth. "If Starbase could only see me now. I bet I'd have the finest Court Martial in navy history."

Zammis swallowed the bite and looked to Davidge expectantly. Its round yellow eyes were huge in its tiny skull, and its expression was both innocent and intense. Suddenly, abruptly, the baby lizard reached out for Davidge, its tiny arms stretching their full length.

"Yeah, you're just doing that 'cause you know it gets to me." Davidge poked another bite of food into the baby's mouth. "Come on, what are you looking at, monster? Eat!"

Zammis looked confused at Davidge's sudden harsh tone. It looked as if it were about to cry.

"Hey! I'm sorry." Davidge hugged the baby close to him. "It's all right, baby. It's all right. From now on, I'll tell all my jokes in a funny voice, so you'll know when I'm kidding. Okay?"

"Gug-gle."

"Yeah, yeah, sweetheart, I know. You're all I have too. We deserve each other, don't we?" He cradled the baby in his arms. "Okay, let that sit for a bit, little guy, and I'll sing to you again." Davidge started rocking the baby gently. "But if you start crying, then I'll have to sing it to you *twice,* so don't say that you haven't been warned."

35

WINTER DISSOLVED into a day of golden light.

The piles of snow were turning into pools of crisp cold water—and surprisingly, the wind felt *warm*.

Davidge woke up, wondering why he was smiling. As he started to stretch, he looked toward the entrance to the cave—and stopped in amazement.

Baby Zammis stood there looking out in wonderment.

"Huh?"

The little creature had crawled out from its bundle of cuca skins and staggered toward the light. Now, it stood erect—a tiny silhouette in the cave mouth, outlined by the bright yellow glare of the day beyond. It was cooing and gurgling with happiness. It had never seen anything so beautiful.

Neither had Davidge.

Grinning like a grandfather, he struggled out of his wrappings. He scooped up Zammis in his arms and carried the little Drac out into the brightness of morning.

The ground was covered with snow, but the sky was clear and the sun was shining.

Davidge turned around and around and around, laughing with joy. He bounced the baby Drac high above him, then hugged the little creature close and whirled it around again. "Look, Zammis, look! We made it! We made it!"

Zammis laughed and blew bubbles of spit.

Davidge laughed and kicked at the snow, then stopped

and turned to face a specific mound of snow. He took a breath, and then he walked over to it slowly. "Hey, god-damn lizard. Look! I kept my word! Here's your baby! Look how big the little monster is getting! It even walks and talks! See, I told you I could get along without you!"

But it would have been more convincing if there hadn't been tears running down Davidge's cheeks as he said it.

36

By the time the last of the meat was gone, so was winter.

By then, Davidge had supplemented their diet with mushrooms, roots, tubers, winterberries, vine flowers and even once—mostly by accident—another cuca. Next time, though, Davidge would have his new bow and arrows ready.

The change of season came so suddenly it almost caught Davidge by surprise, but it wasn't unwelcome. "The planetologists ought to live here on the surface, little monster, if they really want to understand what a bitch Fyrine IV really is."

The little monster cooed in delight. Zammis was filling out at an incredible rate. "Faster than a puppy with three Jewish mothers," Davidge decided.

Using strips cut from Jerry's cuca-coat, Davidge rigged a carrier that he could wear either on his back or across his chest. He had to. He didn't dare leave the baby alone while he foraged for roots and tubers. Zammis loved being carried across the dark mossy slopes below the cave. The moss grew fast; it was thicker than peat and it gave off a delicious warm smell as it burned.

Very quickly, it became a favorite game. Davidge loved to run with the baby slung across his back, making horsey noises and singing the "Lone Ranger" phrases of Rossini's *William Tell Overture*. Zammis laughed out loud when they did this, sometimes hissing like its parent and sometimes cackling in a weird imitation of Davidge's laugh. The latter noise was so startling that the first time Zammis made it, Davidge just stopped and stared at the infant Drac. After that, Davidge found the sound so humorous that he found himself playing with the baby almost every chance he could get.

Indeed, even the sight of Davidge taking down the baby harness from the rock where he usually hung it was enough to start Zammis to giggling and clapping its hands.

"Right! Let's go shopping!" shouted Davidge, scooping up the baby and slinging it into the harness.

Zammis squealed and kicked.

"But, no kicking. You little monster!"

The cautions were wasted. Somehow Zammis had made the association that kicking and squealing would make Davidge whinney like a horse and bounce up and down just a little harder and faster.

"I know, I know. You're Shigan's Revenge. It's all right. I'll get even. I'll teach you how to swear in six different Earth languages. That'll curl their ears in the High Halls."

The Dead Forest was coming back to life. Shafts of sunlight cut the gloom with golden beams, illuminating the ground with a soft, almost misty glow. Davidge walked through the trees in wonder. The world looked like a gigantic cathedral. The distant sound of a running stream sounded like chamber music. The air smelled of flowers and dew.

Davidge found himself humming snatches of Bach and Mozart, and wondered in surprise that he even knew such melodies.

The aeons-old cycle of Fyrine death and rebirth was playing itself out one more time, but this time, there was a witness to its glories. The ancient trunks—those that still stood—were host to a myriad of colored mosses and vines. Silvery things that looked like butterflies or hummingbirds darted among the blue veils hanging from the trees. Thick black snakes coiled slowly through the vines. Davidge was pleased to see how many there were. They were neither hostile nor poisonous, but roasted over a fire, they tasted like chicken.

The weeks passed and Fyrine IV began to reveal more and more of its secrets as spring unfurled. The planet was a bountiful one if a person knew where to look and what to look for.

The last of Davidge's flight suit had long since shredded away, but it was no matter. Davidge was using it for rags now and wearing cuca and snake skins and calling himself Robinson Davidge.

Together, Davidge and Zammis made a pilgrimage to the site of the original cuca-shelter to look for salvage. There wasn't much—a few bits of metal mostly; the rest had rotted away. But it was something Davidge had to do. He had to see for himself.

He noted with satisfaction that only a few bits and pieces of the skeleton remained from the sand-pit predator. Zammis scampered around the clearing like a happy puppy, sniffing and exploring. Davidge watched it carefully. He'd found the remains of Jerry's rifle—totally useless now. He tossed it aside and sat down on a tree trunk.

The little Drac was poking at one of the monster's bones. It picked it up curiously and came running back to Davidge. It held out the bone and peered curiously up into the man's face.

Davidge took the bone and put it aside. He picked up Zammis and held the toddler on his lap. "Well, I'll tell you. It was even uglier than your parent. In fact, it was even uglier than an ugly *Irkmann*. But just the same, the son of a *thing* saved our lives. It was what your parent would have called a miracle. The lizard word is *aelova*. It means 'unexpected opportunity.'"

"Nee-nee," said Zammis. "Nee-nee."

"Mm," said Davidge. "That's right. You're going to start talking in words soon. Well, I tell you what. I'll teach you how to pray in Drac and swear in English. Okay? I'll tell you about Vamma's Assumption in the morning and the Road Runner and the Coyote in the evening. I'll read to you from the *Talman* every afternoon, and in the middle of the night I'll tell you about the two leprechauns and the penguin. It'll be up to you, little monster, to sort the whole mess out."

"Yah, yah!" said Zammis, putting its three-fingered hand on Davidge's face.

"Yeah, yeah," echoed Davidge. He removed one tiny clawed finger from his nostril. "I'll pick my own nose, thank you." He hugged the baby gently. "But you're right—we should try to keep things straight. I mean, we're both skitzy enough as it is."

Zammis gurgled in agreement.

"Yeah, I wonder, who's crazier, little monster? A lizard with an *Irkmann* for a parent? Or an Earthman so lonely he's even willing to raise a Drac baby? What do you think?"

Zammis didn't answer. It had curled up in Davidge's lap and fallen asleep.

"Oh, Jerry—" said Davidge, "—what have you done to me? If you could only see me now." Davidge sighed and added softly, "You goddamn lizard."

══════ 37

DAVIDGE MADE A POINT of singing the baby's lineage every day. Sometimes two or three times. He dared not let himself get sloppy. He dared not let himself forget.

Besides, it was an *anchor*.

He sang the lineage while he skinned the cuca. He sang the lineage while he scraped hides. He sang the lineage while he sewed. He sang the lineage while they foraged. Sometimes, he noticed, Zammis was even humming it along with him.

"Good baby, good little monster. That's the way."

Finally, every night, Davidge sang the baby to sleep with its history. All one hundred and eighty verses of the Jeriba lineage.

After that, when he was sure that Zammis was snoring softly in its bed, Davidge would study the *Talman*. A different section every night. He would sing the chapter softly to himself, practicing its phrases and considering the meaning of each question. There was so much that Jerry hadn't explained to him. He could understand most of the words. But that wasn't the problem. There were cultural artifacts, the equivalents of "Wednesday." Davidge wasn't sure he would ever understand those.

But he gnawed away at the *Talman* like a determined chihuahua working at the leg of a Clydesdale. What little he could understand of the tiny golden book would still be enough to sustain him for a lifetime. Davidge held colloquies inside his head, arguing both sides of every question that the *Talman* raised. He argued from the human side and from the Drac side—what he could understand of it. He argued as a warrior and he argued as a peacemaker. He argued as one committed to his mission and he argued as one who questioned the original purpose of the mission.

The days passed. Zammis continued to grow. And spring faded into summer.

The cave took on a totally new aspect. The snow dunes were gone, leaving behind green lagoons of clear cold water. Where the icicles had been were now bright openings in the ceiling of the chamber, through which golden light poured in. Viney plants dangled down into the cave, festooned with large pink and lavender blossoms. They gave off a rich, fruity smell, sometimes almost overpowering.

The blossoms were actually tiny mouths. The vines caught and ate the little silvery insects. The scent was their lure. Davidge didn't mind; they also grew a sweet, pulpy fruit that Zammis devoured like candy.

One side of the cave was piled high with dried and drying moss. Davidge made a point of always cutting twice as much of the dark purplish peat as he needed. He was already planning for next winter. No more cold nights. And firewood—every time they went down to the Dead Forest, he brought back a bundle of firewood too.

"Hey, squirt! Come here!" Davidge hollered across the cave. He was sewing a small jacket of cuca skin. "Let's see if this fits you."

Zammis came toddling out from the back of the cave. "Squirt?" it said.

"Yeah. Hold still." Davidge held the jacket up against the toddler's body. "I think I'm going to call you Beanstalk. You're outgrowing your clothes faster than I can catch them." He began putting the jacket on Zammis, first one arm and then the other—

"Don't spread your fingers."

"Fin-gers?"

"Yeah, these. Fingers."

Davidge held up his hand and wiggled his fingers. Zammis blinked, looked at Davidge's hand, then placed its own tiny hand against the larger human's.

"Not the same," said Zammis.

"Of course, not the same. I'm an ugly *Irkmann* and you're a little monster—uh, no. Check that. I'm a human and you're a Drac. Look, you have three fingers. One, two, three. And I have five fingers. One, two, three, four, five."

"Zammis get four, five?"

"No."

"Why?"

"Because you're a Drac. And I'm a human. Dracs have three fingers. Humans have five."

"Human?"

"Yeah. Human is me. Drac is you."

"I am Drac? You are human."

"Good! That's right."

"Uncle Willy?"

"Yeah?"

"Will I be human too when I grow up?"

"At this rate, that'll be next week." Davidge frowned at how badly he had underestimated the size of the jacket. "No, you'll still be a Drac."

"Why? Why can't I be a human?"

"Because your parent was a Drac. My parents were human."

"Oh," said Zammis, frowning.

"You don't get this, do you?"

Zammis nodded enthusiastically. "Uncle?"

"Yeah?"

"What is a Drac?"

"Oy vey," groaned Davidge.

"Is that a Drac word too?"

"No, it is not. It's an old Irish expression. And it means *oy vey."* Davidge picked the baby up and carried him over to the pool of water they used for washing. "Now, look in there. What do you see?"

"I see Zammis. I see Uncle Willy."

"Right. Uncle Willy is pink. Zammis is green. Uncle Willy has five fingers. Zammis has three. Uncle Willy has brown eyes. Zammis has yellow eyes. Uncle Willy has big ears. Zammis has tiny ears. Humans are pink and have five fingers and brown eyes and big ears, and Dracs are green and have three fingers and yellow eyes and tiny ears. So I must be a human and you must be a Drac, okay?"

"Okay," said Zammis. It was bored with this game already.

"Good. Okay, let me take this jacket off so I can finish sewing it before you outgrow it."

"Yes, Uncle."

"Yes, Uncle. Yes, Uncle—" Davidge growled to himself. "My mother didn't raise me to be an Uncle." He sighed. "Well, at least I don't have to join the PTA. . . ."

——— 38

THE SOUND BROUGHT Davidge suddenly upright, instantly awake. The first rays of dawn were slanting into the cave.

"What—?" he asked.

It was a hissing in the air.

And then it was a hint of trembling.

Zammis sat up in its bed, staring wide-eyed. "What is it?"

The sound was a low rumble, still inaudible. It started swelling and growing, louder and louder, until the whole cave was shaking. It was a throbbing, overwhelming roar!

Zammis started screaming in terror. Davidge scooped the child up in arms and held it close.

The cave was rattling like it was on wheels. Bits of stone and pebbles came bouncing down from the walls. Davidge ran for the entrance, just in time to see a huge spacecraft come roaring overhead. He turned to follow it as it disappeared over the edge of the world. The rumbling went on and on and on—until Davidge wasn't sure if it was real or just an echo in his ears.

"Oh, shit," he said.

"Oh, shit," echoed Zammis. "Uncle Willy?" The baby had already forgotten its terror. "Was that a spaceship? Like the one you used to fly?"

"Yes, it was a spaceship. No, it wasn't like the ones I used to fly. It was bigger."

"Were there humans inside it?"

"I don't know. I'm going to find out."

Still staring thoughtfully after the ship, Davidge put the child down.

"Can I come too? Uncle, please?"

"Uh, no." Davidge knelt down to face Zammis, putting his hands on the little Drac's shoulders. "It is *very* important that you stay here—*and hide*—until I get back."

"But I want to come too!"

"Zammis, you must stay inside the cave until I get back. You must promise this to me."

"But . . ."

"Promise!"

"I . . . promise."

Davidge didn't like the hesitant sound of that. "Listen to me," he said. "I will not be gone long. I will be back as fast as I can. You must stay here and wait for me— and if you do that, when I get back, I'll teach you all about . . . the facts of life."

"The facts of life?"

"Uh huh. I wasn't going to tell you about football until you were big enough, but if you can prove to me that you're big enough to wait by yourself in the cave until I get back, then you're big enough for the facts of life."

"The facts of life! Okay!" said Zammis. And then, "What's the facts of life?"

"You'll find out when I get back." Davidge headed back into the cave, grabbing a water-sack, a couple slices of dried cuca-meat, his binoculars, and his Robinson Crusoe hat—flat and wide-brimmed, it was as much umbrella as hat. "And don't eat up all the vine fruits or there won't be anything for dessert."

"Yes, Uncle Willy."

39

HALFWAY TO THE CRATER—Dead Man's Crater, as Davidge had begun to think of it—he had a strange thought.

It grew like a cancer until it was almost an audible voice in his head.

Those are human beings! I could go home!

The voice rasped through his thoughts like a dead body in a river. It was shocking and disturbing and ultimately terrifying.

This could be the last day of dried cuca meat and vine fruit.

But he knew—feared he knew—what kind of human beings flew in that ship.

Another thought floated up, unbidden.

But you're a human being too. You have more in common with them than you do with a goddamn lizard. The Drac was your enemy. It shot you down. It killed Joey Wooster. You don't owe it anything.

Yes, I do.

Bullshit. You've been brainwashed. Reading that goddamn book. Now you're thinking like a lizard yourself.

"Shut up," muttered Davidge. He picked his way past the bubbling pools. The crater wall was just ahead. It was only a short climb to the top.

He climbed the rocky slope quickly, muttering and swearing to himself all the way up. "Damn you, Jerry! I really needed this kind of confusion."

He could already hear the noises from within the crater, the distant muffled *thumps* of exploratory seismic tests. The afternoon sun illuminated the steam and smoke rising from the belly of the crater with an eerie red light.

Davidge flattened at the crest and inched forward to peer down into the crater.

The ship stood on the steaming crater floor like a dreadful intruder. Mining machinery had already been lowered from its holds. There was another explosion and a cloud of greasy dust rose into the air.

The work was being supervised by several ragged-looking scavengers. Humans! They swaggered like pirates, shouting orders at their even more miserable-looking workers. There was something about the way those workers moved—

Davidge lifted his binoculars, knowing what he would see even before he focused.

The labor gang was made up of Dracs. They looked beaten. They were covered with dust and dirt and sweat. Their eyes and mouths were clogged with it. Many were skinny and weak from malnutrition. Their skins were dotted with sores and boils.

Davidge watched for as long as he could; then abruptly, he turned and made his way back down the slope, moving as swiftly as he could.

All the way home, the voice in his head was silent.

It was gone. There was no longer any question. Never would be again.

By the time he got back to the cave, dawn was just creeping over the eastern edge of the world.

Davidge stopped before approaching. The cave looked too lived-in. They were probably going to have to disguise the opening. *Listen to me. Listen to what I'm thinking.*

He felt ashamed and disgusted to be a human being.

Well, he would just have to do better for Zammis, that was all. He strode resolutely toward the cave.

Zammis was not in its bed.

Davidge felt his heart lurch. He whirled around, trying to see everything at once. "Zammis! Zammis!" His voice echoed and re-echoed throughout the chamber.

"Uncle—?" the little lizard's voice came softly.

"Here! I'm here!" Davidge shouted.

He turned to see Zammis climbing down from a narrow ledge overlooking the main cave. He noted with approval that it was a ledge that led to an outside opening. Good! The child was smart.

He ran to Zammis and scooped the little Drac up in his arms, in a great bear hug.

"I got scared, Uncle. So I hid."

"You did good, little guy. Real good." Davidge stroked Zammis' head. "And I'm proud of you, very proud."

He carried Zammis over to the campfire and added some moss to it, wondering how much he should tell the little creature about what he had seen in the crater. Probably, the truth would be enough. "All right, little guy," he settled Zammis in his lap, "it's time for a Man-to-Drac discussion about the facts of life."

"The facts? Of life? Now?"

"Yeah, listen. This is very very important. You know what that means? Important?"

"Uh huh." Zammis nodded its head with a very serious expression. "It's like a promise."

"Right. That spaceship—the men in that spaceship are not good men. *Comprendez vous?*"

"*Oui.*"

"They are very very dangerous. If they see you, they will hurt you very badly. They will catch you and hurt you and not let you come home ever again." He didn't know how much of this Zammis was understanding, but he had to tell it all. He had to warn the little guy what he was up against. *"Gavey?"*

"Ae!"

"Tell me what I said."

"You said that if those men see me, they will hurt me. They will catch me and hurt me and I will never get to see you ever again."

"Bueno. Don't ever forget that. No matter what ever happens. If anything happens to me—or anything—don't ever forget that you can *not* trust those men in the spaceship."

Zammis looked up at Davidge. "But why are they bad, Uncle?"

"I don't know. I think it's because they didn't study the *Talman* and didn't learn what *Shizumaat* had to say."

"Didn't they have Uncles to teach them?"

"I don't know if they did or not, but . . . hmmm." Davidge shifted Zammis on his lap. This was going to be a hard one. "It's like this, little guy. They had the opportunity to learn. Every human has the opportunity to learn better. But those men chose not to. You know about choosing, don't you?"

Zammis nodded.

"Good. Well, see, that's what the *Talman* is really about. It's about knowing how to choose. You have to *choose* to be good. You can't just be good automatically, or just because somebody else says you're good. You have to *choose* to do good things and avoid doing bad things. And if you don't choose to be good, then that's just the same as choosing to be bad."

"Did those men choose to be bad?"

"I don't know. Maybe some of them have chosen to be bad, but I think that most of them just don't know any better. I don't think they know they have a choice."

"Could we teach them? You're a good teacher, Uncle."

"Thank you, Zammis, but I don't think it's a good idea to try to teach them. You see, they've been doing bad things for so long that they think they're doing good things. They can't tell the difference anymore. They're . . ." Davidge was having trouble with this. "They're *loco en la cabeza.*"

"Sick in the head?"

"That's right."

"Are all humans *loco en la cabeza?*"

"Sometimes I think so, Zammis, but, no. All humans are not crazy. Someday, maybe, I'll be able to prove that to you. But right now it is very important that you not trust any other human being unless I tell you it's all right. You got that, soldier?"

"Yes, sir. Uncle Willy, sir."

"All right, good. So from now on, whenever we walk or hunt, we will always go in the direction of the rising sun. Never in the direction of the setting of the sun. Is that clear, Zammis?"

Zammis nodded.

"And we'll have to fix the entrance to the cave so it looks like nobody lives here anymore. And we'll have to take care to always approach the cave from a different direction each time so as not to wear a path in the moss. Oh, and we'll have to hide our moss cutting, so it looks like cuca grazing. And—well, we'll just have to watch everything we do from now on." He fell silent.

Davidge held onto the little Drac for a moment longer, until Zammis looked up at him and asked, "Uncle? Are you all right?"

Davidge shook his head. "No, I'm not. I'm very sorry that you had to hear about the bad men this way." He looked into the trusting little Drac's face. "So, I guess I'd better teach you about how good men can be too."

He stroked Zammis' head again. "Shall I tell you about *love?*"

"Love?" asked Zammis. "What language is 'love?'"

"It's human. English."

"And what does it mean?"

Davidge stared out the entrance of the cave, into the beautiful pink Fyrine morning. The words came to him easily. "It means gift. The gift of never-ending gifts. 'I love you' means I give to you because I like giving to you, not because I have to, or even need to, but simply because I choose to. Because it makes my life better as well as yours." Davidge pulled Zammis into a hug. Did Lizards hug? It didn't matter. Humans hugged. "And the way you use the word is like this, little monster: I love you."

"Oh," said Zammis. "Uncle Willy?"

"Yes, Zammis?"

"Do Dracs love too?"

"Of course they do."

"Then I can love you back, can't I?"

"Yes, you can. I'd like that a lot."

"Me too."

40

BY THE TIME AUTUMN had begun to chill the air, Zammis was a head taller and a decade smarter.

They spent almost every day foraging in the Dead Forest now, building up their supplies for winter. Not just wood anymore, but food that could be dried and stored.

"Will the winter really be that bad, Uncle?"

Davidge nodded. "You don't remember, do you?"

Zammis shook its head. *"Nyet."* Abruptly it ran ahead, pointing excitedly. "Look, Uncle! Puffballs!"

At the base of one of the trees was a cluster of giant, white globes. The smallest of the puffballs was ten inches in diameter. The largest was the size of a watermelon.

"They look like footballs," said Davidge.

"Football?" asked Zammis.

"It's a game."

"A Drac game?"

"Nope. A human game. I'll show you." Davidge lowered his pack to the ground and carefully selected one of the puffballs. These things had very thick skins. They needed a little tenderizing. Davidge picked up a couple of sticks and shoved them into the ground to mark a goalpost. Then he paced off thirty yards and shoved two more sticks into the ground.

"All right," said Davidge, turning around to face Zammis. He was holding the puffball under one arm. "The name of this game is football." He pointed. "Now, these trees here are my defensive line, and those over there are your team. They're a little bit bigger than real players, say the Houston Oilers, and a little bit slower. But not much. Okay! You go to your starting position. Go on."

"Okay," said Zammis, and headed down to the far end of the field, a little bit puzzled, but willing to learn.

"Right. Now when I kick off to you, you catch the ball and try to get past me and run between those sticks. That's your end zone. Got it?"

"No." Zammis shook its head.

"Don't worry about it. Just do what I tell you. Here comes the kickoff."

Davidge put the puffball carefully on the ground in front of him, paced backward about twelve steps, "Ready or not, here I come!" He charged down the field and kicked the puffball as hard as he could. It wobbled through the air in an unsteady arc and came down near Zammis with a dusty thud. "Pick it up. Run! Run! Run!"

Zammis grabbed the football and started trotting toward the goal, zig-zagging through the trees. Davidge charged after the Drac, shouting: "The Drac has blinding speed! Look at him weave through that defensive line! But the great Will Davidge is gaining on him . . . gaining . . . gaining."

Davidge grabbed the Drac around the waist and scooped it up into the air, then brought it tumbling and rolling down to the mossy ground. Both were laughing hysterically. They rolled over and over, and then Davidge had the ball and he was up and running in the opposite direction with Zammis chasing after him, squealing and laughing in a wild mixture of exasperation and delight.

"Yes, it's Will Davidge folks! He's heading for a touchdown." He dodged back and forth through the trees, purposely running circles around one of them so he could come up behind Zammis, shouting, "What a runner! What a runner!"

Zammis lunged for him, Davidge jumped sideways and—deliberately—collided with a tree, bouncing backward in an exaggerated fall.

"Oh my God!" Davidge cried, rolling across the ground, still clutching the puffball. "He's tackled on the forty yard line! What a bitter moment for the fans!"

And then Zammis came bouncing down on top of him, still laughing and shouting, "Dogpile on the wabbit! Dogpile on the wabbit!"

"All right. All right!" cried Davidge, prying himself out from under. "First down! I'll show you how to hike the ball. C'mere. You stand there. I stand here, and I shout some numbers . . ."

"Why?" asked Zammis abruptly.

"Why?" Davidge drew himself up fiercely. "Why? You dare to ask *why?* Why Not? That's why! Now, get down again. Here goes. Seventeen, thirteen, twenty-two, *hike!*" He jerked the ball backward, then turned to chase Zammis down the field.

Zammis was giggling as it ran, shouting, "It's the Drac's game now, folks. The Drac is running. The Drac has got the ball."

"Watch out for that tackle!" shouted Davidge. "Pass it! Pass it!"

Zammis tossed the puffball and then ran into a tree. Davidge leapt and grabbed the ball out of the air. He charged down the field, shouting, "The pass is completed! What a play! The game goes to the Drac team! The crowd is going wild . . . the fans are pouring into the stadium. Oh my God, it's a riot!"

Davidge charged over to Zammis, hoisted the little Drac onto his shoulders and ran in a great circle around the field in a joyous display of victory.

Afterwards, as they sat and rested on a log, Davidge carved up the puffball. He handed a piece to the Drac.

Zammis bit and chewed loudly. "I like this game," it announced.

"Yeah, it's a good game," Davidge replied. "Of course, you don't normally get to eat the ball. That's kind of a bonus. And I've simplified the rules a little for the conditions here—smaller teams and so on." He reached over and ruffled Zammis' nonexistent hair. "You're a good kid, kid."

Abruptly, Zammis said, "Uncle, I have been thinking."

"Mm hm, about what?"

"About those humans you saw. You said they had Dracs working for them."

"That's right," Davidge said cautiously. Where was this heading?

"Couldn't it be like you and my parent? Couldn't they be friends?"

Davidge shook his head. "I wish that were true, little guy. Why do you ask?"

Zammis made a hissing, sighing sound. "I have never seen another Drac, Uncle. I want to know what a Drac looks like."

"You've seen your reflection, many times. That's what a Drac looks like."

"I don't like what I look like. I don't want to be a Drac. I want to be a human like you."

"Hey! Zammis!" Davidge reached out and put a hand on the child's shoulder.

"I wish I had five fingers!" Zammis held out its hands before it.

"Hey! Hey!" Davidge shouted, sudden anger in his voice.

Zammis shut up abruptly.

Davidge turned the little Drac so they were facing each other. "Don't you talk like that. You are the one hundredth and eighty-first generation in one of the oldest and most noble lineages of all Draco. You are Jeriba Zammis! My line can only be traced back three generations, but yours! My God, Zammis! Wait and see! Someday, you'll go home and you'll see!"

"I don't want to go to Draco. I want to go to Earth and meet Mickey Mooze!"

"Well, maybe we can do that too. But, I made a promise, Jeriba Zammis, that I would take you to Draco and recite your lineage in the High Halls, so you could take your rightful place in your family. I made a promise to your parent, Shigan, that I would do this thing, and I'm not going to break that promise, Zammis. I'm not. That's all there is to it."

Zammis didn't answer immediately. It was staring at its hands. After a moment, it raised its eyes to Davidge's. "What was Shigan like?"

"Shigan was . . ." Davidge fell silent. He didn't know how to answer the question. "Zammis, your parent was my friend. Shigan saved my life. More than once. And I saved Shigan's. And," Davidge suddenly realized something, and grinned out loud, "your parent gave to me because it wanted to give. And I gave to your parent because I wanted to. Your parent gave me one of the greatest gifts of all, this *Talman*. I have learned so much from the study of it. More than I ever knew was possible. Shigan was very very smart. On the day we leave this world, I will put this *Talman* around your neck and you will wear it back to Draco, and then every Drac you meet will know who you are and what a great parent you had."

"I want to meet other Dracs now," said Zammis.

"I wish there were Dracs you could meet," replied Davidge.

"Uncle Willy, are you really certain that those men in the crater are *meshugah?*"

"Sweetheart, they are worse than *meshugah*. They are—" Davidge searched his memory for an appropriate obscenity, *"merde. Dreck.* You know what that is? That's *kiz*. They are the *kiz* of *kiz*-eaters."

"Yicch," said Zammis.

"Right," said Davidge. "Yicch."

41

Six days later, Zammis was gone.

Davidge woke late and sat up wondering why it was so quiet in the cave.

Maybe Zammis was using the toilet, a place in the back of the cave where the water flowed down into an underground stream. No, the Drac wasn't in the back of the cave.

"Zammis?" Davidge wasn't alarmed, yet. But he was getting there.

He stepped out of the cave and hollered as loud as he could, "Zammis! Zammis! *ZAMMIS!!*"

There was no answer.

Davidge frowned. He turned and went back into the cave. Zammis's heavy coat was gone. And so were Davidge's binoculars.

Shit.

Davidge realized with a sinking heart exactly what the little bastard had to be thinking. He took his bow off the wall, a cuca-skin quiver of arrows, and a water sack.

He set out at a run. He didn't know how much of a head start the little Drac might have, but if he kept his pace up he had a good chance of catching up to it before it reached the crater.

Oh, God—I hope I'm in time.

No. He wouldn't let himself think that way. He headed rapidly down the slope. One hundred yards walking, then one hundred yards running. One hundred yards walking, then one hundred yards running. For as long as it took.

The sun climbed into the sky.

Zammis had left long before dawn.

The Drac had been thinking about this for a long time and planning it for almost a week.

And today was Wednesday. It was that simple.

It wasn't hard to find Dead Man's Crater. It dominated the horizon. Its plume of smoke and steam was a landmark on the western horizon.

By the time the sun had reached zenith, Zammis was standing in the crater's shadow. The little Drac had found its way easily through the maze of bubbling pools.

The faint sounds of machinery—clanging noises and metallic high-pitched shrieks—floated out of the crater. The Drac's eyes widened in wonder. It quickened its pace.

Zammis made its way quickly up the slope. The steam was thick. Zammis hadn't realized how close it was going to have to get, but it was almost there and it was going to see a real Drac! It wasn't going to come all this way for nothing.

Zammis peered over the edge.

The huge scavenger rig sat like a tarantula in the crater. It cast a huge black shadow over the toiling figures below. Zammis laughed with excitement and lifted the binoculars to its eyes.

For a moment, it didn't understand what it saw.

Yes, those were Dracs. They were bigger than Zammis expected, but they had the same kind of faces as the one that reflected in the water. And they had three-fingered hands. And—

But they looked so thin and so . . . unhappy.

As Zammis watched, one of the scavengers walked

over to one of the Dracs and—seemingly without reason—punched it to the ground.

Zammis gasped in horror.

The Drac fell and didn't get up. The other Dracs
glanced over quickly, and then kept on working.

Tears welled up in Zammis's eyes. It buried its head
in its hands and began to cry in deep, gulping sobs. It
had never seen anything so horrible in its life.

How could Uncle Willy stand it? How could he let
such evilness exist in the world?

Zammis felt betrayed.

After a while, the little Drac began to work its way
down the side of the crater. It was time to go home and
apologize to Uncle Willy. And . . . And . . . Zammis didn't
know what else to do. But something had to be done.
Something. What was it Uncle Willy always said? "Intelligent life takes a stand."

The steam from the boiling pools was thicker now.
Zammis threaded its way carefully across the rocky
ground. Abruptly, it stopped, confused.

A figure came out of the steam. A man. A towering
human thing with steel-gray hair. Huge. Bigger than Uncle Willy! The man had evil blue eyes and a lean hard
look. He was wearing a huge black pistol on his belt.

"Yeep," said Zammis, and took a step back.

The man was as surprised as Zammis.

Zammis turned to run—and found his way blocked
by another human. This one was younger, thick bodied,
barrel-chested. He had a face that was both vicious and
simple-looking. This man was wearing a long deadly-
looking rifle on his shoulder.

"Hey, Johnny! Look what we caught! A cute little
woggie if I ever saw one."

"Looks a little small to me, Stubbs."

Zammis's gaze flickered back and forth, looking for a way past the two men.

"I wasn't thinking about usin' it for work, Johnny."

Zammis didn't understand what the man meant by that, but the little Drac didn't like the way the man said it.

"Yeah. That's a good idea too," laughed Johnny.

Zammis was paralyzed with terror—and then Stubbs stepped forward, reaching—and Zammis leapt aside quickly, turning to run—

Johnny stepped in to block the way. "Come on, woggie! Come on! Runabout! Runabout!"

Zammis whirled again, and there was the monstrous Stubbs blocking the other retreat. "Boo!" Stubbs grinned nastily and laughed.

The two men circled the little Drac, blocking its escape. Each time Zammis made a break one or the other would block the way.

"Hey, it's a fast one!" said Johnny. "How do you suppose it got here."

Behind Zammis, Stubbs gestured at Johnny, pointing to the left. Johnny lunged for the left, Zammis ran to the right—straight into Stubbs's thick arms. "Gotcha woggie!"

Zammis struggled futilely in the man's strong grasp. "I dunno," said Stubbs, suddenly concerned. "Better look around. See if its Daddy is lookin' for it." Stubbs started to shift his grip—

—and Zammis twisted in the man's arms, suddenly raking its three sharp talons across the scavenger's fat cheek.

Stubbs howled in pain and let go of Zammis, who hit the ground running.

Stubbs's hand came away from his cheek bloody. There

were three deep gashes carved into his flesh. The big man's expression turned crimson with rage. He sputtered incoherently, then took off running after the little Drac.

But Zammis was too fast. All that football with Uncle Willy had been good practice for this! The Drac dodged and darted across the rocky ground, moving like a wild animal. Stubbs came lumbering after.

Zammis glanced back—the sight was terrifying. The huge human was a monster from Hell!

Zammis started up a steep, muddy slope that rose toward a jagged ledge of rock. On one side the ground dropped away into a depression filled with several hot, bubbling mud pools. When Zammis looked back again, the man was closer. Gaining.

Johnny appeared on a rise behind Stubbs. "Hey, Stubbs! Hot damn! Woggie's really got you hot and bothered." He giggled insanely and put his rifle to his shoulder. "Don't worry! I'll slow him down a bit."

But before Johnny's finger could tighten on the trigger, a stinging arrow suddenly pierced through his neck. Johnny looked surprised, then annoyed, then dead. He sank to his knees, then flopped sideways. He slid down, making a loud gurgling noise in his throat. The body toppled into a boiling pool of mud and disappeared quickly.

A moment later, Davidge came climbing up where Johnny had been standing. Looking up the slope, he saw Stubbs pursuing Zammis through the swirling steam. Davidge took a deep breath and went charging after.

Zammis was already up to the top of the ledge; the Drac's body was covered with the cloying mud. Before the little Drac could catch its breath, Stubbs was already scrambling up the slope after him. "I've got you now, you slime-eating lizard! You're going to be glad you've only got three fingers on each hand 'cause I'm going to pull them off one by one!"

Stubbs advanced slowly toward Zammis, choking with rage.

The little Drac was frozen with fear and exhaustion, and then suddenly, it saw—

"Uncle! Help me!"

The English words caught Stubbs off balance. He stared at Zammis, confused. "What the—?" He yanked his pistol from its holster, whirled and fired at Davidge, missing him only by inches.

Davidge leapt sideways, disappearing into the steam.

Stubbs took a step forward, squinting, peering down the slope. "Son of a bitch!" He started cautiously forward—

—and then, just as suddenly as he had disappeared, Davidge reappeared. Behind Stubbs. With an arrow notched and aimed straight at the man's chest.

Stubbs turned—and snorted.

"Who the fuck are you, Robin Hood?"

"You got it, asshole."

"Uncle!" Zammis ran toward Davidge, not realizing, coming between the two men and blocking Davidge's aim.

"Zammis! No!" Davidge dodged sideways to get a clear shot at Stubbs, but Stubbs was already firing. Davidge spun, hit in the arm. His foot slipped from the ledge and he slid, clawing for a hold, one arm useless. He caught himself and—

It was the ledge above the lagoon again. Davidge flailed wildly—

Stubbs appeared above him, grinning murderously. He kicked away Davidge's hand—and Davidge fell, disappearing through the steam.

Zammis' scream followed him all the way down. "Uncle! Uuuunnnnncle!!"

Blam! Blam! Stubbs fired two shots down through the

steam, not even aiming, just pointing his gun in the general direction that Davidge had fallen. Maybe he'd hit him, maybe he hadn't. It didn't matter. At the bottom of the slope was boiling mud.

"Robin Hood, my ass!" he laughed. Then he turned again to Zammis—

══════ **42**

"DAVIDGE? CAPTAIN DAVIDGE?"

Davidge opened his eyes. The face staring down into his was human. Young. Too young. Clean-shaven. Smiling. Dressed in green. A med-tech.

Instinctively, Davidge reached for his knife. It was gone. He was in a hospital gown. In a bed. And the gravity was different, lighter. Everything smelled *good*—even the blond man.

"Captain? I'm Major Steerman," said the man. "I'm your doctor. How are you feeling?"

Davidge didn't answer the question. "Where are we?"

"You're on a medical relief vessel, headed back to Earth."

"Earth?!"

"Uh huh. The war is over. You're going home."

Davidge felt confused. There were too many questions. "Over?" Too much was happening here, too rapidly.

"You were brought in by a survey team," continued Steerman. "You were in pretty bad shape. They didn't expect you to make it. But you fooled us all. You're too tough to kill, Captain."

"Survey team?"

"The United States of Earth and the Dracon Chamber have established a joint commission to supervise the colonization of the disputed planets. The team was mapping an abandoned scavenger site when they found you."

"Zammis!" Davidge tried to sit up. "What happened to the scavengers?"

"I don't know about the scavengers. Who's Zammis? You've been talking to this Zammis almost continually since you were brought in."

"I have?"

Major Steerman smiled. "Yeah, about football and Mickey Mouse—and uh, the leprechauns and the penguin. I have to tell you, not a lot of it made sense, Captain. You were babbling in six different languages, including one that even sounded like Drac. Who was Zammis? Your navigator?"

Davidge's eyes narrowed. "Don't try to con me, Major. You know who my navigator was."

Steerman smiled apologetically and looked at his clipboard. "Jerry Wooster?"

"No. *Joey.*"

Steerman corrected his file. "Dead?"

"Yeah," Davidge admitted. "We crashed. What happened to the scavengers? Where did they go?"

Steerman shrugged. "Who knows?"

"What about their prisoners?"

"You mean the Dracs? They're being returned to their own planet. It's in the treaty. What else would we do with them?" Captain Steerman studied Davidge for a moment. "Zammis is a Drac?"

"Yeah," Davidge admitted.

Steerman's eyebrows went up a notch. "I'll bet there's quite a story behind *that*. You want to share it?"

Davidge studied the man. He decided that he didn't trust him. Too smooth. Too much he wasn't saying. "No," he said.

"Okay. Fine with me." The doctor switched off his

clipboard. "If you change your mind, you'll find me more than willing to listen."

"You writing a book?" Davidge muttered.

"As a matter of fact, I am." Steerman looked pleased.

"Well, you can leave this chapter out." Davidge rolled over and faced the wall.

43

A WEEK LATER, Davidge was knocking on Steerman's door.

"Come in."

Steerman looked up from the paperwork. "Davidge?" He looked surprised.

"I got a question."

Steerman nodded and thumbed his console for privacy. They wouldn't be interrupted. "Sure."

"How do I go about finding Zammis?"

Steerman pursed his lips thoughtfully. He made a tent of his fingers in front of him while he considered his words. "Why don't we make this conversation off the record, Captain."

Davidge narrowed his eyes. "What are you trying to tell me?"

"Just that I think that's a very bad idea. I've gone over your record. As it stands right now, you're a war hero. You've got a lot of back pay coming to you. Probably a couple medals, and I wouldn't be surprised if you didn't find yourself in a parade or two when you hit groundside." Steerman lowered his hands to the desk. "Don't screw it up."

"Don't . . . screw it up?"

Steerman nodded slowly. "It probably wouldn't look too good for a war hero to admit to having a Drac friend—

and to raising a Drac baby. You can imagine what some people might think about that."

"So, you do know."

"We had an interpreter listen to the tapes of your delirium. She didn't understand everything, but she understood enough. And we ran some names through the computer. The Dracs have been giving us lists of MIA's. There's no Jeriba Zammis on any of the lists, but there's a Jeriba Shigan, a pilot, missing in action the same time you disappeared. Zammis would have been the next in the line. It's not too hard to figure out the rest. Jerry is short for Jeriba, right?"

"Yeah, right. So what?"

Steerman clucked his tongue inside his cheek. "Well, you kept talking about this Jerry. At first, we thought that Jerry was a man."

"And that Jerry and I . . . ?"

"Mm hm." Steerman shrugged. "That actually would have been okay, Captain. You wouldn't have been the first war hero bent that way; and the gay community would have taken good care of you. But a Drac lover is something else entirely."

"Jerry and I weren't lovers. The Dracs don't take lovers."

Steerman didn't look convinced. "Couldn't prove it by the way you talked on the table. You know, you're lucky I'm your doctor. I'm not like a lot of other guys who might have drawn your case. They'd have opened your skull just for the fun of it. You could have disappeared into a rubber room, Captain. But, ah, I've been studying the Dracs, sort of as a hobby, for a long time—"

"Yeah, I'm sure."

"—so I like to think I can be more sympathetic than most. I really do want to help you, but you're going to have to cooperate with me in return. Look, I'm on your side, but frankly, Captain, you have to realize that you have the potential to become a first class embarrassment. You make people nervous. I thought I might be able to give you some help and perhaps make everything work out to everybody's advantage."

"We're talking about the military's public image, right?"

Steerman admitted it. "That is a consideration too, yes."

"All right," Davidge conceded. "I'll listen. What do you want?"

"Not a lot, really. You're a hero, remember. All we want is for you to act like one. I don't think you need me to spell it out."

Davidge said, "Yeah, I know what you want. I'm not a trouble-maker, if that's what you're worried about. I'm mission-oriented. I'm after results."

"Good. I'm glad to hear that," said Steerman, sitting up—a signal that he was preparing to end the meeting.

Davidge ignored it. He remained planted in his chair. "Okay, now it's my turn."

"Beg pardon?"

"We're playing 'Let's Make A Deal'—aren't we? Now I get to ask for something. What happened to Zammis?"

"I'm sorry. I don't know," said Steerman.

Davidge eyed him suspiciously. "Is that really the truth?"

"Captain, you can think whatever you want of me. But I'm not a liar. I said I don't know. And I don't." Steerman added in a gentler tone, "But I did take the liberty of making some inquiries—very discreetly, of course."

"And—?"

"The Dracs have no record of any Jeriba Zammis being repatriated."

"What?"

"Hear me out, Captain, I'm not through." Steerman had to raise his voice.

Davidge sat back in his chair.

"There is no record on *our* side of any Jeriba Zammis either. Zammis may have died at the hands of the scavengers, or it may still be alive. It may be on its way back to Drac, or it may be already there. But there is simply no record of it anywhere. No paperwork. Not on our side, not on theirs."

"That's not possible."

"Yes, it is," Steerman said, watching Davidge closely. "Think about it."

Davidge shook his head. "I don't know what you're talking about."

Steerman said, "You really don't know?"

"Tell me."

"Okay." Steerman began slowly. "You know how the Drac lineage system works, I presume."

"Yeah."

"You know about the Drac *Bar Mitzvah* too?"

Davidge ignored the bad joke. He simply nodded. "Yeah. Before a Drac can take its place in the family, its parent—or a qualified representative—has to sponsor it before the High Council. Someone has to read the child's lineage, to introduce it to the society."

"Right. 'Today I am a Drac,' and all that." Steerman looked grim.

"Would you get to the point, please?"

"Do you know what happens to a child without a sponsor?"

Davidge thought about it. He shook his head. "Jerry never said."

"It doesn't exist," said Steerman. "It has no rights. At best, it's a piece of property. If a family thinks a child will not become a credit to the line, they can have it destroyed and try again with the next baby. It's the name that's important to a Drac, not the child."

Davidge kept his expression stoney. "You're wrong," he said. "That's a total misinterpretation. The *Talman* says..."

"Yes?"

"Nothing."

"Captain, you're anthropomorphizing the Dracs. That's a bad mistake. A Drac baby matures in three and a half years. The Dracs don't have the reproductive investment in a single child that a human parent would. A Drac doesn't think anything of abandoning an inferior or a defective child. Its loyalty is to its parent, not its baby. We've seen this in the prison camps. Dracs have given birth and killed their children immediately to keep from dishonoring the line."

"To keep their children from being *slaves!*"

"Same thing," shrugged Steerman. "To a Drac, being a slave is dishonorable."

"No! They do it to save the children! They think we're slave-eaters!"

Steerman looked surprised. "An interesting theory, Captain. But it doesn't change the facts. Jeriba Zammis doesn't exist. Not yet. The Zammis you raised has probably already been destroyed. I'm not sure how the lineage system handles such an occurrence when the parent is already dead, but I do know that a family would rather end its line than let the line be dishonored. No, I'd bet money on it—your Zammis is probably long gone."

Davidge stood up. His throat hurt from holding back his anger. "You think you know about Dracs? You don't know shit. Did you ever hear this one? 'Intelligent life takes a stand!' I made a promise, and I'm going to keep it."

"It's a waste of time, Davidge."

"It's my time to waste." Davidge stopped at the door. "Don't worry. I'm not going to embarrass the service, but I am going to keep my word. Because my honor as an *Irkmann* is all that I have left."

Steerman stared out the open door and sighed. This one was going to be tough. He'd have to think of something else.

44

DAVIDGE'S PARENTS SEEMED LIKE STRANGERS. They were glad to have him home again, and at the same time, they were just a little bit uneasy whenever he walked into the room.

They didn't understand. On their side, it looked like this:

"Why don't you call Jackie Thorne? Her mother says she'd love to hear from you."

"Hey, son, how about you and I going down to the bowling alley tonight?"

"Willy? Will you be home for supper? I'm making your favorite, stuffed cabbage."

Davidge tried *once* to make them understand. Only once.

His Dad had interrupted him quickly.

"You don't have to talk about it, son. The doctors explained it to us. We understand."

"That's just it, Dad. You *don't*. Not really. I don't think any human being can understand this unless..."

Their faces were blank, uncomprehending.

"Never mind." Davidge got up and left.

The bright yellow sun seemed alien to him. The air was too thin and everything smelled mechanical. He didn't belong on this planet anymore.

He had mustered out with $48,000 in back pay.

It wasn't enough.

Passage to Drac—assuming you could get a passport—was nearly $200,000.

There had to be a way.

Miracles. Expect a miracle, Jerry had said. Depend on it. Not a very logical way to run a life. But then, Willis E. Davidge's life had been anything but logical.

Davidge sighed and turned around and headed for home.

His mother met him at the door. "Willy, dear, while you were gone, this package came for you."

"Huh?" Davidge popped it open. It was from Dr. Steerman.

Inside the box were his dog tags, a handful of photographs, a couple of medals, his knife and some other odds and ends. One item was wrapped up in brown paper. Davidge didn't recognize it.

There was a note enclosed:

"Captain Davidge," it began. "I told you that I've made a hobby out of studying the Drac culture. There's much that I still don't *gavey*. But I do understand what you meant about keeping promises. When I became a doctor, that was a promise to spend my life healing others. I am returning your personal effects to you because I think it will speed the process of your own healing. I hope you will think of me as a friend, or at least as a sympathetic ear always willing to listen. If I can be of any further service to you, please don't hesitate to call on me. I can be reached at Edwards Air Force Base."

"Hmp," said Davidge. He tossed the note aside and poked through the box again. The knife he would keep. He glanced only briefly at the photographs. Not a single one of those people was still alive. Morse. Cates. Arnold.

He unwrapped the item in the brown paper.

It was his *Talman*.

He stared at it, unbelievingly, emotion swelling up in his chest. "That son of a bitch," he grinned. "That lousy son of a bitch."

45

DAVIDGE HID INSIDE the *Talman* for a month.

He read constantly, chanting out the hard passages until he knew them by heart. Sometimes, what he read made him angry. Sometimes, the tears came unbidden to his eyes.

But one day, he read a verse that didn't make sense at all and he had to sit down at his desk and try to translate it into English. The closest he could come up with was, "The head is filled with unfinished conversations—things that have not been said. The head carries them around forever, collecting clutter like a *trimble* collects *kipple*. Finishing the conversation completes the miracle."

Terrific. What the hell did that mean?

Finishing the conversation completes *what* miracle?

Davidge went to the phone and punched up Edwards Air Force Base. "Major Steerman, please."

"One moment. May I say who's calling?"

"Davidge. Will Davidge."

"One moment."

Davidge waited, wondering what he was going to say.

And then Steerman's face appeared on the screen in front of him. "Hi."

"Hi, yourself."

Steerman glanced at his watch. "You held out longer than I thought you would. I expected to hear from you two weeks ago."

Davidge shrugged. "I guess I'm not too good at saying thank you," he admitted.

Steerman grinned out of the screen at him. "There's really no need."

"Well." Davidge was embarrassed. "Thanks anyway for returning the *Talman*. It means a lot."

"Besides," said Steerman, "I have an ulterior motive."

"Oh?"

"Nobody I know can read more than a few words of it. In fact, nobody I know has ever seen a copy of the *Talman* before."

"I'm not surprised. You wouldn't. It's one of the holiest items in the Drac culture. The owner of the *Talman* is the custodian of the lineage."

Steerman nodded. "That's what I found out when I began checking around. That little artifact is extraordinarily valuable. For you to be carrying it—well, Jeriba Shigan must have had a lot of respect for you, Will Davidge."

"Yeah, I guess so," Davidge admitted wryly. "That's why Shigan always called me, 'ugly *Irkmann*.'"

"Well, I am impressed. And that's what I wanted to ask you about. Do you want a job?"

"Doing what?"

"Writing a translation."

"For who?"

"Take your pick. I can get you a Federal grant, if you want. Or, if you'd rather not be working for the government, you can probably auction off the rights for some pretty fancy money to any of a half-dozen publishers."

"You're kidding!"

"Nope. I mentioned you to my agent. I told you I was writing a book. You would have been one of the most interesting chapters—except my agent had a better idea. A Drac dictionary and a translation of the *Talman*, the

Drac holy book. He checked around. There are publishers interested. And it's an exclusive, because you're the only human being on Earth who can do the job. We could be talking as much as a half million golden dollars."

"Excuse me," said Davidge. "There's something wrong with this phone. It sounded like you said a half million dollars."

"No, I said a half million *golden* dollars. Noninflatable. Davidge, are you there?"

"I'm here. I'm just trying to figure out where you hide your wings and your halo under that uniform."

Steerman laughed. "You'd be surprised. Now, get a pencil and write this number down—"

46

SIX MONTHS LATER, Davidge was on a starship headed for Drac.

The Curtis Agency had licensed exclusive rights to the Davidge translation of the *Talman* and the Davidge Drac–English dictionary to a special partnership of three international publishing houses for what was euphemistically called, "an unspecified amount of money." Translation: The ten percent that the Curtis Agency took out of the deal was more money than most writers earned in a lifetime. There was also an open-ended option on Davidge's war biography, including film rights.

Davidge hired three assistants—an Egyptian rabbinical student, a Zen-Buddhist scientologist, and a left-wing Jesuit priest—to supervise the transcribing. He read to them every day from the little golden book and then got out of the way while they argued over what they had heard. If the three of them, with six opinions between them, could come to an agreement on the meaning of the passage, then Davidge knew that he had communicated the sense of the chapter clearly.

In the meantime, he had Steerman pulling a few strings behind the scenes to obtain copies of the records of all scavenger vessels operating anywhere near Fyrine IV. *The Scurvy Bastard*—appropriately named, thought Davidge—had lost its charter nine months *before* Zammis had stumbled into their grasp.

The same survey ship that had discovered Davidge

lying on the edge of a boiling mud pool had also carried a contingent of Federal Marines who placed the crew of *The Scurvy Bastard* under immediate arrest for violating the terms of their labor contract.

Steerman translated it for Davidge. "Don't you believe it, Will. The truth is, we're trying to save a little face here. The scavengers were operating under the umbrella of public approval. The military knew what was going on. But now that the war is over, we all get to pretend we were 'good Germans.' I owe you an apology on this one." Steerman didn't look happy.

"Forget it," said Davidge. "What happened to the prisoners?"

"That one's a little harder," Steerman checked his notes. "The prisoners were transferred to a holding camp on West Thule. From there, they were dispersed to their home planets. According to this, there were three hundred POW's in the dispersal and twenty-three unnamed children, who were born in the labor camp. If I read this correctly, all the children were transferred to Drac."

"Thank you!" shouted Davidge. "If you were here in this room, I'd kiss you!"

"It's all right. You can owe it to me," grinned Steerman and signed off.

On the day that Davidge completed the first draft, he booked passage for Drac. "For additional research," he said.

The first half of the journey was aboard the *U.S.S. Henry Kissinger*. Davidge transshipped to a Drac vessel at Far South—a rocky little mudball, distinguished only by the fact that it was equidistant between Earth and Drac, and that it was the site of the recently concluded truce talks.

Once aboard the Drac ship, Davidge spent most of his time in his cabin, but since the Drac stewards refused to serve him, he had to take his meals in the ship's lounge with the rest of the passengers.

He sat alone, listening to the comments about him from the other booths. For the most part, he pretended that he didn't understand the Drac language.

"Must we eat in the same compartment with the *Irkmann* slime?"

"Look at it, how its pale skin blotches, and that evil-smelling thatch on top. Feh! The smell!"

Davidge ground his teeth and kept his glance on his food.

"It defies the *Talman* that the universe could create a creature as corrupt as that."

That one was too much.

Davidge stood up and approached the table where the three Dracs were laughing boisterously. He held up his *Talman* and sang politely, "Excuse me, but I can't find anything at all in the *Talman* to justify that last comment. Could you show me chapter and verse?"

The three Dracs stared at him, astonished.

"It speaks," gasped one.

The second Drac rang for the steward.

The third gulped loudly and began to stammer an apology, "Excuse my companions. We did not know you were civilized."

"It's all right, I didn't know you were civilized either. I certainly couldn't tell it from your comments." Davidge bowed politely. "You may tell your companions for me that if the elders of their village had seen fit to sterilize their defective children properly, their offspring would not presently be embarrassing themselves in public."

He returned to his table while two of the Dracs struggled to hold the third one down.

The next day, the stewards began serving Davidge in his cabin.

——47

THE JERIBA ESTATE was surrounded by a high stone wall.

Davidge stared at it from a distance and wondered how he would be greeted.

According to Dracon law, once he stepped onto the Jeriba property, he was under the rule and domain of the Jeriba clan. They could—legally—claim his life as payment for the damages he had inflicted on the Jeriba clan.

"Jesus Christ, Jerry," Davidge said to himself. "I am never again going to promise anything to a goddamn lizard." He started for the gate.

The guard at the gate gaped as Davidge approached. It had never seen an *Irkmann* before.

"I want to see Jeriba Zammis," Davidge sang to it.

The guard blinked in surprise. Then, it hissed, "Wait!" and disappeared into an alcove behind the main gate. It returned quickly and resumed its post, staring malevolently at Davidge.

Davidge sighed and waited.

Through the gate, he could see the huge stone mansion that Shigan had described to him on several different occasions. It was bigger than Davidge had imagined.

In a few moments, another Drac emerged from the mansion and walked quickly across the wide lawn toward the gate. It nodded once to the guard then stepped up to Davidge and eyed him suspiciously.

Davidge stared right back. The Drac was a dead ringer for Jerry.

"You are the *Irkmann* that asked to see Jeriba Zammis?"

"My name is Willis Davidge."

The Drac studied the man. "I am Estone Nev, the sibling of Jeriba Shigan. My parent, Jeriba Gothig, will see you." The Drac turned abruptly and headed back toward the mansion. Davidge followed, feeling both heady and nervous.

He was ushered into a large room with a vaulted stone ceiling. Jerry had once said that the house was over four thousand years old. Davidge believed it now. He was led to a low dais, supporting a large uncomfortable-looking chair. A throne? Davidge glanced around quickly. The room was very formal-looking.

"Wait here," said Nev. It disappeared behind the chair, and came back a moment later, leading an older, slower-moving Drac.

Davidge bowed politely. "Jeriba Gothig, I am Willis Davidge."

Nev took up its place beside the throne, as if waiting for its parent to sit. Gothig glanced at the chair in annoyance, then stepped down off the dais and approached Davidge. Its yellow eyes searched Davidge's face. "Who are you, *Irkmann?* Why do you ask for Jeriba Zammis? What do you want here?"

Davidge sang, "I have come to keep my promise to Jeriba Shigan."

"Jeriba Shigan is dead—has been dead for six Dracon years. Shigan died in the battle of Fyrine IV. What is your scheme, *Irkmann?*"

Davidge turned from Gothig to Nev. Both of the Dracs were examining him with the same look of suspicion.

Davidge cleared his throat and sang softly, "Shigan

was not killed in the battle. We were stranded together on the surface of Fyrine IV and lived there for a year. Shigan died giving birth to Jeriba Zammis. I raised Zammis until..."

"Enough! Enough of this, *Irkmann!*" Gothig roared. "What do you want? Are you here for money, to use my influence for trade concessions? What?"

"I want *nothing* from you!" Davidge roared right back. "I am here to see Zammis!"

"There is no Jeriba Zammis! The Jeriba line ended with the death of Shigan!"

"That is not..." Davidge stopped himself. He turned away long enough to compose himself, then turned back to Gothig again. "Noble Gothig, forgive me for my impertinence. I know that it is wrong to inquire of a host's breeding, but it is essential that I ask. Are you telling me that Jeriba Zammis has not yet been presented to the High Council, or are you saying that no child destined to become Jeriba Zammis has been returned to Drac? Or are you saying that the child has been...destroyed?"

Gothig looked enraged. It turned to Nev and hissed softly. Nev hissed back grimly. Gothig turned back to Davidge. "There is no child. There *was* no child. The Jeriba clan is ended. Now, get to the point of your scheme, *Irkmann!*"

"The Jeriba clan is not ended. Shigan died giving birth to Zammis. Shigan entrusted me with the care of Zammis. And Shigan—" Davidge took a deep breath. "—*appointed me custodian of the Jeriba lineage!*"

For a moment, Davidge was afraid that Gothig was going to have an apoplectic fit. The old Drac was struck speechless with horror and rage. It turned to Nev and gestured feebly with one hand. "Have this...this *thing* removed from the house."

Davidge quickly fumbled the *Talman* out of his shirt,

pulling it over his head and holding it out so Gothig could see what it was. "Jeriba Shigan taught me to read the *Talman.*"

Gothig took the book from Davidge's outstretched hand. The Drac's own hand was trembling. It opened the *Talman* reverently, satisfying itself that it was indeed the *Talman* of the Jeriba clan. Then, abruptly, it looked up at Davidge, eyes still hard. "You have defiled my house, *Irkmann.* I will have it cleansed. You have defiled my name and my lineage, *Irkmann.* I will forgive that too. But now you have defiled the *Talman* and the words of *Shizumaat.* That I cannot forgive."

Gothig turned to Nev. "Have it killed."

Davidge gulped. There was only one thing left to do. He cleared his throat and began to sing: *"Son ich stayu, kos va Shigan, chamy'a de Jeriba, yaziki nech lich isnam liba, drazyor, par nuzhda. . . ."*

Gothig froze in its tracks. As did Nev.

Davidge sang and they turned to stare, astonished. Davidge sang and tears welled up in Gothig's eyes. Davidge stood in the house of Jeriba and sang the lineage of the Jeriba clan, from Jeriba Ty, through all one hundred and eighty verses, concluding finally, sadly, proudly, with the deeds of Jeriba Shigan.

When he finished, he waited for Gothig's reaction. The old Drac had sunk to the floor and knelt there throughout most of Davidge's recitation. Now, it stood up and looked at Davidge with eyes filled with confusion and wonder. "If you are a schemer, *Irkmann,* then you are the best of your species. And if you are not, then you will be an honored guest in this house."

Davidge bowed. "I am here, Jeriba Gothig, only to keep my promise to Jeriba Shigan—to stand with Zammis before the High Council and recite the lineage. Now, where is Zammis?"

48

GOTHIG ARRANGED QUARTERS for Davidge on the grounds
of the estate — not in the main house, but in a guest house
set back away from the mansion. Davidge guessed that
it was a question of propriety. It simply wouldn't look
right for an *Irkmann* to live in the house proper.

It didn't matter. Davidge was glad to be out of the
city anyway. The continual barrage of insults and hate
stares was exhausting. The important thing was to find
Zammis.

The first thing that Davidge had to learn about Draco
was that Dracs moved at their own speed and any attempt
to hurry a Drac usually produced the opposite result.

Davidge quickly learned to keep his mouth shut and
let Gothig do the inquiring. Gothig — Davidge discovered — had the kind of influence that only presidents and
movie stars had on Earth.

After several days of inquiries, Gothig announced that
it was sending Davidge and Nev to the Chamber Center
in Sendievu, Draco's capital city, where they were to
meet with a representative of the Joint Survey Commission, a Drac named Jozzdn Vrule.

Jozzdn Vrule was a thin-looking Drac with a pinched
face. It studied the letter of introduction that Gothig had
given Davidge with a puzzled frown. "Where did you
get this, *Irkmann?*"

"The signature is on it," Davidge said.

The Drac looked at the paper again. "You claim that Jeriba Gothig gave you this?"

"Isn't that what I said? I thought I said it. I felt my lips moving when I said it." The sarcasm was wasted.

Nev stepped in quickly. "The information in that letter is correct. We want to know what happened to the child destined to become Jeriba Zammis."

Jozzdn Vrule frowned. "Estone Nev, you are the founder of a new line, are you not?"

"I am."

"Would you found your line in shame? Why do I see you with this *Irkmann?*"

Nev's expression hardened. "Jozzdn Vrule, if you contemplate walking this planet in the forseeable future as a free being, it would be to your profit to stop working your mouth and start finding the child."

Jozzdn Vrule looked down and studied its fingers, then returned its glance to Nev. "Very well, Estone Nev. You threaten me if I fail to hand you the truth. I think you will find the truth a much greater threat."

"No one is ever threatened by the truth, Jozzdn Vrule," Nev said. "—Except those who invest in lies."

The Drac sniffed and scratched a note on a piece of paper. "We shall see. There were twenty-three children returned from Fyrine IV. Seven of them have been claimed by their families. Two have been destroyed. Two more have died of the treatment they received at the hands of the *Irkmenn.*"

"And the other twelve?"

"Unclaimed. Or unclaimable." Vrule's expression was sour, even for a Drac. "You will find the children at this address, and you will curse the day that I gave you this."

Nev looked at the paper without expression. Carefully, it folded the note and placed it in a pocket. "The Jeriba Clan and the Estone Clan both thank you for your service,

Jozzdn Vrule. And the spirit in which it was offered will
not be forgotten."

Jozzdn Vrule flinched. But to give the Drac its due,
Vrule still bowed and showed them out with civility.

Out on the street, Davidge turned to Nev. "What was
on the paper?"

"A terrible grief," said Nev.

"Will you share it with me?"

Nev turned hard yellow eyes on Davidge. *"Irkmann,
on the day that you entered my life and my parent's, you
brought us anger and fear. Today, you have given us
grief. Tomorrow, we shall pursue this and be plunged
into despair. Is that what you would have us share?"*

"Estone Nev, sometimes you look and sound so much
like Jeriba Shigan that it is difficult for me to remember
that you are not Shigan itself; but know this, Shigan
offered me friendship freely, and in return I gave Shigan
my word that I would see Zammis brought before the
High Council. Whatever horror there is, whatever pain,
whatever despair, it is rightfully mine as much as yours."

"Irkmann, you are ugly," Nev said, surprising Davidge immensely, "but you have honor. More honor than
I would have expected from an *Irkmann.* If my sibling
found you worthy of its friendship, than I will do no
less. What is the *Irkmann* custom? We shake hands?"

Davidge found himself deeply moved by the offer.
"Ae!" He held out his hand.

And there on the streets of Draco's capital city, Estone
Nev shook hands with the ugly *Irkmann.*

49

GOTHIG LOOKED AT THE ADDRESS on the paper and flinched. "It is a House of Despair."

"I'm sorry," said Davidge. "I don't understand."

Gothig smiled. "Ahh, as well as Shigan taught you, I see that my child still left holes in the wall for others to patch. *Irkmann,* grief is the most inevitable of all emotions, is it not?"

"Such has been my experience," Davidge admitted.

"And as such, grief is a natural part of living. It is neither bad nor good. Do you know that too?"

"I do."

"Good. Then you must also know that grief is a finite emotion. It cleanses and it heals and then it departs; do you see that as well?"

Davidge nodded.

"But despair . . ." Gothig wagged a finger at him. "Despair is not finite. Despair is grief without cleansing, without healing. It is grief that does not end; grief that does not see an end."

"Yes," said Davidge. "I *gavey.*"

"Do you?" Gothig looked stern. "Do you *gavey* a House of Despair?"

Davidge considered the implications in the term. "It is not a place of healing?"

"No. It is not."

"Then it is . . . a place where those who cannot be healed are kept. Is that correct?"

Gothig nodded sadly.

Nev spoke up then. "It is worse than that, *Irkmann*. If a child cannot be healed, then its family will have it destroyed. Those that are kept in the House of Despair are either unclaimed, or unclaimable. Because they are not claimed, there is no authorization to destroy them. Their despair goes on forever."

Davidge sat down weakly. He wanted to bury his head in his hands. The feeling of despair was infecting even his soul now. "Just one question, Nev. Do any come back from the House of Despair?"

Nev didn't answer.

Gothig said, "We are not a callous people, *Irkmann*. None are sent to the House of Despair if there is a chance of healing. I have never heard of one returning from there."

Davidge looked up at the two Dracs. "So, what you're saying . . . ?"

"The best that we can hope for, Will Davidge, is to end the pain of the child."

Davidge heard the words, but he couldn't accept the meaning behind them. He stood up again. "Please do not think me rude, Jeriba Gothig, but I will not accept that as the only solution. If you don't have the faith, I do. I will claim the child. Jeriba Zammis will be healed."

"You are very certain of yourself, *Irkmann*."

"Why not? Today is Wednesday."

══════ 50

THE HOUSE OF DESPAIR was set away from the city. It was a half day's journey.

When they got there, the two Dracs and the man from Earth, the gates were barred. Gothig announced itself at the gate and they waited.

Shortly, the director of the House came out to meet them. It was a haunted-looking Drac, and it bowed deeply and respectfully. "Jeriba Gothig, Estone Nev, I would advise you to turn around and go home. Otherwise, what you will see inside here will haunt you forever."

"If I do not enter," replied Gothig, "the thought of what I did not see will haunt me forever. Open the door."

"On your own heads, be it then. Come this way."

Inside, it was Bedlam.

It was Hell.

The House of Despair was a colony of imbeciles and defectives, the damaged and the insane. Most of the Dracs there were older ones. They sat and stared into space with vacant eyes, or they sat and drooled on themselves, or they wandered, babbling through the halls. Others, behind locked doors, were screaming or crying or moaning. Some were violent, hurling themselves against the doors of their cells. Others had to be restrained to keep from biting and hurting themselves. Some simply sat and soiled themselves. Some acted out arcane rituals of movement and words. And some didn't move at all.

Davidge was horror-struck.

He turned to the director of the House. "How can you let these things happen?"

"Irkmann, do not speak to me. Where *Irkmenn* infest, disease, despair and death follow as certainly as night follows day, as pigs follow *kiz*. This is *your* work here, *Irkmann!"*

Nev grabbed the director and spun it around.

Gothig raised one hand warningly. "You will *not* be rude to a guest of the Jeriba Line!" it thundered. "Now bring us to the child!"

The director didn't flinch. "Very well. Very well. We have tried to protect the Jeriba reputation. We tried!"

"The reputation of the Jeriba Clan is not your responsibility," said Gothig stiffly.

"I beg your pardon, nobility," said the director. "But it has been our experience that most families don't even want to deal with the disgrace of claiming a child in order to destroy it." The Drac bowed apologetically. "It was our understanding . . ."

"Never mind what you understand! Bring us to the child now, or you will know the wrath of the Jeriba Clan!"

"Aae! I will lose my position here for doing this, but I will lose it willingly to see you disgraced, you pompous *kizlode!* You want to see the being that calls itself Jeriba Zammis? See it and weep!"

The director led them outside, to a peaceful blue lawn under a darker blue shade tree. To a bench where Jeriba Zammis sat silently staring at the ground. Its eyes never blinked. Its hands never moved.

Gothig frowned. Nev hesitated. But Davidge stepped forward eagerly, "Zammis?"

The Drac did not react.

"Zammis. Don't you know me?"

The child was much bigger than the last time Davidge had seen it, almost as tall as a teenager. Slowly, it retrieved its thoughts from a million miles away and raised its yellow eyes to look at the *Irkmann*. It blinked twice, but there was no sign of recognition. "Who are you?"

Davidge gulped hard and squatted down in front of the young Drac. He put his hands on its arms and shook them gently. "Hey, little monster, it's me. Remember your Uncle Willy? Remember?"

The Drac weaved on the bench, looking back and forth, anywhere but the *Irkmann*. "No, I don't know you." It lifted an arm and waved to an orderly. "I want to go to my room. Please, let me go to my room."

Davidge grabbed Zammis hard then. "Zammis! Look at me!"

"No! No! Please!"

The orderly came rushing up, dropping a large yellow hand on Davidge's shoulder. "Let it go, *Irkmann!*"

"Zammis!" Davidge turned futilely to Nev and Gothig. "Please! Say something to it!"

The orderly pulled a sap from its pocket, then slapped it suggestively against the palm of its hand. "Let it go, *Irkmann!*"

Gothig turned to the director. "Explain this."

"I said we tried to protect the Jeriba name. This one, this unclaimed child was brought to us professing a *love* for humans. A love, mind you! It spoke in human words. It preferred the human language! It even said it wanted to be a human instead of a Drac! We have seen many perversions here, but this—" the director shuddered. "This staggers the mind. The Lower Chamber wanted to protect you from this scandal. Would you wish this known across all of Draco? That the Jeriba Line has spawned a thing that craves humanity?"

Davidge stood up then. He towered over the director. "What have you done to Zammis, you goddamn lizard? Shock therapy? Drugs? A lobotomy? What?"

"You think it would be happy as an *Irkmann vul*—a human lover?" sneered the director. "We are making it possible for this one to function in Drac society. You think this is wrong?"

Davidge turned back to Zammis. The child was trying to follow the conversation, but confusion was flickering on its face.

Confusion swept over Davidge as well. He was remembering his own treatment at the hands of human beings. The reactions of the other patients on the hospital ship as the rumors about him circulated. His quick and quiet discharge from the service. Even the strange looks he had caught his own parents giving him when they had thought he wasn't looking.

The question was obvious. Was it fair for him to ask Zammis to be a misfit in its own culture?

Should he have even come?

"I don't know," Davidge said. "It's not my place to judge."

The director of the House turned to Gothig. "You understand, Jeriba Gothig, don't you? We would not subject the Jeriba Line to such a disgrace. We felt it was better to keep it here unclaimed, and see if we could cure its sickness. And if we could, then perhaps . . . the Jeriba Line could continue. Was this presumptuous of us? That we would try to protect your line from scandal? Was it wrong?"

Gothig turned away, shaking its head. Nev moved to comfort its parent.

Davidge—frustrated, almost crazy—squatted down in front of Zammis again. He held the Drac's hand between his own, interlacing their fingers.

Zammis looked at him for just a moment then, fear flickering up in its eyes, then just as quickly it dropped its glance again. With its other hand, it started prying Davidge's fingers gently open, one at a time. "One ... two ... three—"

Davidge was about to let go, when Zammis abruptly said, "—*four ... five!*"

"Zammis!" Davidge's heart leapt.

Gothig and Nev turned and stared. The director looked horrified. The orderly hissed.

Zammis blinked and looked up. "Uncle—?" It placed one clawed hand on Davidge's cheek. "Uncle? Why are your eyes so wet?"

51

ESTONE NEV TOOK CHARGE of having Zammis released to the custody of the Gothig clan. The director of the Institute was reluctant to sign the papers. "I do not wish to be known as the one who turned loose a disgrace such as this."

"You will mind your tongue when you are discussing the heir to the Jeriba lineage," Nev said. The Drac pushed the release form at the director. "Now, sign it. Or you'll be lucky to get a position shoveling *kiz*."

The director signed the paper sullenly. As it handed the paper back, it said, "Apparently, this particular perversion is a genetic weakness in the Jeriba line. We should have destroyed the child."

Estone Nev took the paper and looked it over carefully. "Thank you for your signature. And then be thankful that you are not worth killing or your blood would already be flowing across this floor." He left the room quickly, as if something smelled bad there.

Zammis was already sitting in the back of the car, between Gothig and Davidge. The little Drac was turning confusedly back and forth between its grandparent and the *Irkmann*. "I am not supposed to love *Irkmenn* anymore. Am I? Was I wrong? Why did they tell me not to love? Can I start loving again? Are you really my grandparent? Uncle? Uncle Willy? I'm sorry I ran away. Please forgive me. Is that why you let the *Irkmenn* keep me?

They hurt me, Uncle. Please forgive me. You won't give me back to the bad *Irkmenn* again, will you? Grandparent, please don't let Uncle Willy send me back to the bad *Irkmenn*. Uncle Willy, please don't hurt me."

"Zammis..." Davidge started to say, but Jeriba Gothig stopped him with a look.

"Irkmann, you have brought shame and pain to the Jeriba lineage. Do you now wish to bring further disgrace? Is this the individual you wish to bring before the High Council?"

Davidge didn't answer for a long moment. "I made a promise to Jeriba Shigan. I have to keep my promise. If Zammis has been damaged, then the damage was done by Dracs, not by me."

"Some of the damage was done by *Irkmenn!* Slavers."

"That is true. I'm sorry. Both of our species are guilty then. There is enough guilt for all of us. We can either wallow in it, or we can attempt to undo the damage. Which is it to be Jeriba Gothig?"

Now it was Jeriba Gothig's turn to fall silent. "When you came into my house, you brought me anger. And hope. Then you brought me despair. And then hope again. Now, there is only pain and still you offer me hope. No wonder your race is so evil. You will not stop while there is pain left to bring."

"If you will not help the child, then I will. Send us back to Fyrine."

Gothig glared at Davidge. "I will never let it be said that an *Irkmann* did what Jeriba Gothig would not. We will help the child together."

Davidge put his hand on Zammis's shoulder then. "Zammis. Listen to me. Nobody is going to hurt you. Never again. Never. I promise you that. I promise on the grave of your parent. Look at me, Zammis. Do you believe me?"

Zammis turned to Davidge and searched the *Irkmann's* face. Its expression was both hopeful and frightened.

"I came back for you, Zammis. It took me a long time, but I didn't forget, and now that I'm here, nobody is going to hurt you."

Zammis's expression cleared then. Finally, it dared to let itself believe. The little Drac hugged its Uncle Willy as hard as it could and hung on fiercely. "Uncle! Uncle! Uncle Willy!"

On the other side of the car, Jeriba Gothig looked annoyed and uncertain—and just a little bit hopeful.

52

ELEVEN MONTHS LATER, Jeriba Gothig made a decision.

It was a hard and painful decision, and a joyous one as well.

"I have decided," Jeriba Gothig announced, "to submit the name of Jeriba Zammis to the High Council." That was the joyous part.

The hard and painful part came when petition was actually handed to the High Council.

The members of the Council passed the document among them, blinking in surprise as they read it through.

This was very irregular. Very irregular *indeed*. The custodian of the line was not even related. In fact, the custodian was totally unknown to the Council.

Finally, Ivvn Lar, one of the junior members of the council, spoke. But instead of the routine response that Gothig expected, the Drac lord looked curiously across at Gothig and asked, "Who is the custodian, this Davidge of the clan of Willis? We have no recognition."

"Willis of the clan of Davidge," corrected Gothig, "is the legally appointed custodian of the Jeriba line. The Davidge line is very short. Perhaps that is why you do not know of it yet."

"Yes, it says all that here. But *who* is this Willis of the clan of Davidge. Let the person rise."

Gothig bowed deeply. "I regret to inform you that

Willis of the clan of Davidge was not allowed to be admitted to these halls."

"And why is this?" frowned Zanz Kandanz, the senior member of the council. "No legal custodian has ever been denied access to this hall."

Gothig bowed again. "Such may have been the case in the past, but the custodian of the Jeriba line *has* been denied access."

The members of the council looked at each other in consternation. If what Gothig said was true, then an extraordinary breach of etiquette had occurred. If Jeriba Gothig demanded it, an extraordinary apology would be necessary. Perhaps even a dishonorable suicide.

"Where is the custodian now?"

Gothig hesitated. This was a delicate moment. "The custodian waits with the candidate."

Kandanz replied with equal hesitation, "Is the custodian still willing to appear?" If Gothig demanded an apology for this insult, this council would be irrevocably stained.

Gothig said, "My lords, the custodian wishes nothing more than to recite the lineage and be free of the responsibility. The custodian will appear, if its right to appear before this council is not challenged again."

The lords of the council shifted in their seats. It was the motion of a lizard being removed from a hook. Only Zanz Kandanz did not relax. "You use the word 'challenge', Jeriba Gothig. Is there any reason why the custodian should be challenged?"

"No reason that I can find," Gothig replied. "But there may be some who will think that this custodianship is irregular."

"And why is that?"

"Willis of the clan of Davidge is an *Irkmann*."

The members of the High Council flinched in horror

and disbelief. Ivvn Lar rose to its feet in dismay. *"Gaak!* Jeriba Gothig, if this is a joke, it is in extremely rude taste. If it is not a joke, then even a dishonorable suicide will not spare your nobility!" The council member glared down at Gothig.

Zanz Kandanz tapped the table with a short fan of polished rods. Ivvn Lar looked embarrassed and sat down. The council recomposed itself and looked to Jeriba Gothig with distaste, waiting for the rest of the unpleasant request.

Gothig met the gaze with equanimity. "I repeat my request, my lords. I request permission for the legally appointed custodian to approach the council and recite the lineage." Gothig bowed and then continued the ritual request with deliberate underlining of its meaning, "If there is any reason why this cannot be, please state it now."

The council members were trapped.

If a council were to deny the petition, it would be almost as big a scandal as if they were to allow it. Petitions were *never* denied. Wars had been fought for the right to lineage. If now—in the new age of enlightenment—a council were to attempt to deny a lineage, the Equity would not be satisfied until either the council or the petitioning clan had dishonorably suicided. And even then—

The horrifying part of the whole disgusting situation was that Jeriba Gothig's request was absolutely *legal*. The *Irkmann* had met all the conditions of the custodianship. It had taken responsibility for the *Talman*, the lineage and the child. All of the conditions of the petition were in order.

The situation was—to put it mildly—unprecedented.

The council was trapped. They could allow the *Irkmann* to recite the lineage, and dishonor their culture, in which case they would not be allowed even a dishonorable suicide. Or, they could disallow the petition and just as surely dishonor their own lineages; but at least, in that circumstance, their suicides would be legal.

Shizumaat!

Nowhere was it written that the sponsor of the child had to be a Drac.

The only hope was that perhaps, somehow, Jeriba Gothig could be persuaded to withdraw the petition.

Or, at least, allow it to be ... set aside somehow.

It would mean the end of the Jeriba lineage, of course, but it would also mean the end of this particular dilemma. If the petition were withdrawn, then it would be as if it had been never submitted, and the members of the council could then petition for an honorable suicide in response to the insult they had suffered.

A proper study of the petitions, and the appropriate forms of honorable suicide, might take as long as thirty or forty years. And no other forms of death—other than accidental, of course—could be petitioned while the original request was still being considered.

Hm.

This situation might have an acceptable conclusion after all.

53

THE AMBASSADOR'S CAR arrived for Willis Davidge the following morning.

Two men in black suits were there to deliver a formal invitation to Willis Davidge to attend an audience with the Official Representative of the United States of Earth to the Dracon Chamber. Davidge met them on the lawn in front of the Gothig household, flanked by Gothig and Nev. The two men were built like boar wrestlers. And they were quite insistent about his attendance. In fact, they told him, he would not be allowed to refuse. Davidge nodded. He doubted he could win such a fight.

Instead, he grunted in acknowledgment. "Am I under arrest?"

"The United States Government has no police authority on Draco," said the shorter of the two men. Shorter by one-quarter inch. "However, you as a United States citizen are under the protection of the United States Embassy here—and you are advised to attend this audience, *for your protection.*"

Davidge nodded. "Yeah. I can read between the lines as well as anybody." He looked from one to the other. "I request a legal witness to attend with me."

For the first time, the two men looked nonplused. They exchanged a quick glance. "That is your right, of course."

The second man said, "We were informed you were traveling alone. Who is your witness?"

Davidge grinned and pointed. "Estone Nev."

"A Drac? Don't be stupid!"

"There's no law that says a legal witness has to be human, and on this planet, a Drac witness is more legal than a human one. Estone Nev, or I'm not going."

Nev looked startled and whispered quickly to Davidge, "What iss going on, *Irkmann?*"

"They're trying to kidnap me. If you come with me, they won't dare. They'll have to release me. If they can hold me incommunicado, then there's no one to recite the lineage. I think your High Council is really upset with me. This is how the Terran government is trying to resolve it."

Nev turned to Gothig and explained the situation. Gothig nodded slowly, in understanding. "But, Nev, you are under no obligation to the act in the service of the Jeriba clan."

"I do this out of loyalty to my parent," Nev replied, "as well as to my sibling. If an *Irkmann* can demonstrate such honor as this one has, I can do no less."

Gothig looked delighted. So did Davidge; if his grin got any wider his face would have split in half. "Estone Nev, I'm going to have to teach you about Mickey Mooze. Let's go."

They were taken directly to the United States Embassy. The car pulled up to an indiscreet entrance on the side of the building. Davidge and Nev were escorted immediately to a small private lounge.

They exchanged nervous glances. Nev started to speak, but Davidge stopped the Drac in midphrase. "No," he cautioned. "I'll bet the room is . . ." Davidge scratched his head in confusion. How did you say "bugged" in

Drac? "Filled with listening devices," he concluded lamely. "They're probably listening to us."

"Oh," said Nev. Then: "Who is this Mickey Mooze, you keep talking about?"

"I'll tell you later."

The Ambassador came in then, frowning, followed by a frozen-faced secretary.

The Ambassador was a petite woman, but there was very real anger in her face. She was clearly in no mood for this particular problem. Her secretary was another one of those tall men in black suits.

"Willis Davidge?" She shook hands perfunctorily. "And this is Estone Nev, right? Is that the correct pronunciation?"

"Yes," said Davidge. "Nev doesn't speak English."

The Ambassador studied Davidge. "Very unusual, Mr. Davidge—to request a legal witness and then bring one who doesn't speak English."

"For what I need witnessed, English isn't necessary."

"Yes, I see," said the Ambassador. She glanced at Nev distastefully. She didn't mind Dracs. She minded the situation. She turned back to Davidge. "You underestimate me, Mr. Davidge. And you overestimate your own importance."

"Be that as it may," shrugged Davidge. "You wanted to see me?"

"I did, yes. To ask you one question." The Ambassador looked Davidge straight in the eye and asked, "Just what in the bloody hell are you trying to do? Start the war again?"

"Madam Ambassador, what I am *going* to do—there is no such thing as *try*—is keep my promise and recite the Jeriba lineage in front of the High Council."

"Do you understand the political ramifications of what

you are attempting? Do you realize that if you continue, you will force the entire Drac Chamber into a—we don't have the exact equivalent, but think of it as a constitutional crisis. If you persist, you will undo everything, and I mean *everything*, that we have been working so hard to achieve with these people."

"Madam Ambassador, I believe I *gavey* the circumstances far better than you or anyone on your staff."

The Ambassador looked annoyed. "Mr. Davidge, I know your history. You have had some extraordinary experiences and my experts have found your primitive translations to be quite adequate. But you are an amateur messing in a field where even trained professionals refuse to speak with certainty."

"Precisely," agreed Davidge. "I have certainty. Your people do not. Because they can't see past their own dogma. The fact is, the Drac culture is *not* as brittle as you people believe. Dracs are *not* as dogmatic as human beings. The Dracs are, however, more expressive of their feelings. They will dramatize their upsets quickly, get past them and then get on with life. We humans insist on pretending we're not upset and then go home and kick the dog. Now, you tell me who's got a healthier approach?"

"I am not here to argue with you, Mr. Davidge. I am here to officially request that you terminate your actions on this planet."

"No," said Davidge.

"Perhaps you don't understand. It is a *request* of your government that you stop what you are doing because it will destabilize the Terran–Drac relationship. We are both speaking English, aren't we?"

"It sounds like it to me," said Davidge. "By my dictionary, a request means I have a choice. I can say no. No."

"If you do not accede to this request," the Ambassador said politely, "you will have your passport revoked. If you remain here on Draco then, it will be at your own risk. You will no longer be entitled to the protection of the United States of Earth."

"Frankly, Madam Ambassador, I'd rather trust the Dracs. I've *seen* what the United States of Earth calls protection. Have you?"

"Mr. Davidge," the Ambassador said coldly. "Mistakes have been made on *both* sides. What we are trying to do now is avoid making any *more* mistakes. Are you going to cooperate or not?"

Davidge turned to Nev and explained the situation. Nev frowned thoughtfully. "As legal custodian of the Jeriba clan, you are guaranteed the protection of the Dracon Chamber. To that, I will add the personal protection of the Estone clan. I am certain that my parent will add the protection of the Jeriba clan as well."

Davidge nodded. "I thought so." He didn't even have to think about what to do next. He turned back to the Ambassador. "Do you want me to surrender my passport now? Or do you have some official rigamarole to go through first?" He proffered the tiny blue folder.

The Ambassador made no move to take it. "If I accept your passport, the Dracon Chamber can have you killed without fear of repercussions from this government. Do you understand that?"

"I understand it, Madam Ambassador, yes. And I am willing to take that chance." He handed over his passport. "Is there anything else you want?"

"No," she shook her head, "there isn't. But, just to satisfy personal curiosity, I would like to know *why* you are doing this."

Davidge shrugged. "Why not?"

"I beg your pardon?"

"It's like jazz, Madam Ambassador." Davidge stood up to leave, Nev stood up too. "If you have to have it explained to you, then you don't understand it."

54

THE DAY AFTER THAT, a secretary of the Dracon Chamber came to call on Jeriba Gothig. It was purely a social call, of course.

The Dracon government could not, of course, officially request that a lineage withdraw its petition. Nonetheless, if Jeriba Gothig were to withdraw the petition for the recitation of the Jeriba lineage, the Dracon Chamber would be quite pleased.

No Dracon citizen, of course, would ever refuse a request from the Dracon chamber, but since this was not a request, Gothig had, of course, refused. The petition would *not* be withdrawn.

That is unfortunate, said the representative and left politely.

In the next three days, two members of the High Council committed dishonorable suicide, and a third council member had itself sterilized rather than continue a line that had been dishonored.

Eleven days after that, Jeriba Gothig submitted its petition a second time.

The remaining four council members considered their options and retired to study the *Talman* and the four thousand volumes of interpretation in the libraries. We'll get back to you on this. Don't call us, we'll call you.

That night, Davidge came to Jeriba Gothig and asked if they might speak privately. Gothig nodded and ordered tea. They sat quietly and breathed the vapors of the steaming herbs for a long time before Davidge finally spoke. He said to the elderly Drac, "I have not asked you this, and it occurs to me that I should consider your wishes in the matter before we press it to its conclusion. Do you wish to withdraw the petition?"

Gothig looked at the *Irkmann*. "Is it *you* who wishes to withdraw? If so, why do you push the burden of responsibility onto me?"

Davidge took a breath. "I guess I didn't realize what I was starting, here. I have placed you in an uncomfortable position. If you must share the burden of my consequence, my lord..." Davidge used the honorific deliberately; Gothig ignored it, "then you should also carry your part of the choice."

Gothig smiled. "It would not be the first time the Jeriba Line has been outspoken. Well, perhaps this is the first time the Jeriba Line has been *this* outspoken." The old Drac pointed to a thick stack of law books. "This is a matter that would justify the placing of one's hand on one's sword. Do you understand what I mean? We do have the right. I can find no argument here to stop you, *Irkmann*. And I wish I could, because it would be the easier way out. And the law would be intact. But," admitted Gothig with a wry expression, "equally, I am glad that I cannot. I admit that I would not be as dismayed as most to see you succeed."

"That does not answer the question," said Davidge.

Gothig laughed. "You dance well, *Irkmann*. But it is still your choice. It always has been. And you know it. Or you would if you had studied the *Talman* as much as you say you have. You have triggered an avalanche. Now you must ride it. We all must ride it, or be crushed before it. There is no force as powerful as a promise that insists on being kept."

Davidge bowed his head deeply. "You show me the truth, my lord, and I am both honored and humbled. I will not doubt again. I thank you for enlightening me."

"On the contrary, *Irkmann*—what is the correct address? Ugly *Irkmann?* On the contrary, it is I who should thank you for enlightening me."

══════ 55

THIRTEEN DAYS LATER, Jeriba Gothig stood again before the High Council. Beside him stood Estone Nev. And this time, behind them both, stood the candidate and the custodian. The candidate was dressed in a white robe. The custodian wore blue.

Jeriba Gothig stepped forward to address the council. The old Drac spoke slowly, but with great force behind its words.

"I am told, my lords, that many believe that if I submit this petition a third and final time, that it will unleash great chaos in this world. I humbly submit, my lords, that this is the truth. Many do *believe* that this petition contains the seeds of destruction.

"I do not.

"I do not believe that the simple recitation of a lineage, as specified in our own laws, can bring about the downfall of a world. I do not believe that the fulfillment of a promise, as specified in the *Talman,* can bring about the end of our traditions.

"What I know goes beyond mere *belief*. I know that if we do not honor our own laws and traditions, then those laws and traditions shall be as the dust on the wind. It is the job before us, here today, to do nothing less than demonstrate once again the wisdom of our ancestors and the truth of our ways.

"I ask you to consider simply this: What is the great

crisis that so many of us seem to fear? That an *Irkmann* should stand here and honor a Drac's last wish? I tell you freely, that I carry no great affection for *Irkmenn* of any kind, and yet, still I find myself standing here, willing to defend to the death this *Irkmann's* right to recite.

"Many have died, on both sides. And the wounds still hurt, on both sides. There is much pain. More than enough for all of us to hurt for years to come. But is yesterday's pain a valid reason for creating more pain today? It is time the war was truly ended, my lords. It is not enough to end the war in our skies, we must end it in our hearts as well.

"By our standards, the *Irkmann* is ugly, and its habits are crude and uncivilized. But it has honor. It has kept its word. So far. Now, the only thing keeping it from the completion of its task is the High Council of Draco. I ask you, my lords: Is this how we demonstrate the honor of Draco? By violating the honor of another? I think not. No. I think not.

"The *Irkmann* wants only to complete its promise to Jeriba Shigan. My lords, when you ask it why, it quotes from the *Talman*. 'Intelligent life takes a stand!' If an *Irkmann* can quote from the *Talman*, then perhaps it is time for the High Council to listen. Perhaps it is time for the Chamber of Drac to take a stand as well! After all, as the *Irkmann* would say, 'Today is Wednesday. Anything can happen!'"

Jeriba Gothig stepped forward, bowed, and placed the petition on the table before the High Council.

The council members looked at each other. Three of them looked beaten. Zanz Kandanz picked up the petition and studied it carefully.

At last, the senior member of the council spoke. "You speak well and movingly, Jeriba Gothig. It is clear that your lineage has much to offer the Dracon Chamber. It will truly be a great loss to our world to see the Jeriba lineage ended here. You say that you do not believe that this recitation will bring chaos down upon our heads. And yet, our history has shown that chaos, like an avalanche, can be unleashed by the movement of a single stone. What if you are wrong, Jeriba Gothig? What if you are mistaken? It is not just the job here to honor the law and the traditions of Draco; it is the job of this Council to protect the clans of Draco as well."

The senior member of the council appeared to choose its next words carefully. "Jeriba Gothig, as you know, there is no law by which to prevent the *Irkmann* from singing. And yet, just because there is no law, that does not make an action right. Everything you have said is logical; but if logic were all that were necessary for the practice of justice, then there would be no need for a council; we could have the job executed by a machine.

"Just as you and your servants have studied the law, seeking a solution for this dilemma, so have the members of this council and our servants. If there is no law to prevent the *Irkmann* from singing, neither is there a law to compel this council to listen. The *Irkmann* may recite in this hall for as long as it chooses. We shall return when it has completed its task."

Zanz Kandanz stood up then, so did the other three members of the council. They started for the door.

Estone Nev leapt to its feet to protest. If the council members left the chamber without officially adjourning, then the hearing was still officially in session, but if there were no council members to witness the recitation of the lineage—

Jeriba Gothig stood up quickly and placed its hand on the arm of its child. "No. Wait," said Gothig. "Zanz Kandanz!" called Gothig.

The senior council member stopped where it was. "Yes, Jeriba Gothig?"

"I honor your wisdom. Let me honor you further by inviting you to attend the recitation of the Jeriba lineage. And you, Ivvn Lar, will you join us as well? And please, Mamu Niyon, accept this honor also. And Phelger Carb, please?" Jeriba Gothig bowed and waited.

The four council members were paralyzed where they stood. To refuse Gothig's invitation would be a terrible insult. Jeriba Gothig would be justified in requesting their deaths. The three junior members traded nervous glances. What would Zanz Kandanz decide?

The senior council member let out its breath slowly. "I believe, old Gothig, that you have finally achieved what many have sought, but few have accomplished. You have outwitted the High Council. You have my compliments. Indeed, I would be honored to see that a lineage as clever as yours is continued."

Zanz Kandanz returned the bow of Jeriba Gothig. A moment later, so did the other three council members.

Jeriba Gothig turned around to face Willis Davidge. "You wanted to sing, *Irkmann?*"

"Yes, Jeriba Gothig. I wish to sing."

David took the hand of the Drac who wished to become Jeriba Zammis and the two of them stepped forward to face the four remaining members of the High Council of Draco.

Davidge looked each one of them in the face, straight on and unashamed. Then he turned to Zammis and lowered the hood so that Zammis' face could be seen by all. He lowered his own hood and then turned to face the chamber.

Oh, Jerry, let me make you proud!

Willis E. Davidge took a breath and began to chant:

*"Son ich stayu, kos va Shigan, chamy'a de Jeriba, yaziki
nech lich isnam liba, drazyor, par nuzhda...."*

And as he sang, the tears began rolling slowly down
his cheeks. Davidge didn't even try to wipe them away.
He just kept on joyously singing. The expression on his
face was beatific.

He had kept his word. Jeriba Zammis had come home.

Someday Zammis would stand before this council and
present Jeriba Ty. Ty would bring Jeriba Haesni to this
place. Haesni would bring Jeriba Gothig. And after that
... Gothig's child would be called Shigan.